OPEN BOOKCASE

COLLECTED STORIES

ENGLISH CREATIVE WRITING GROUP
FRANKFURT

FRANKFURT'S OPEN BOOKCASES

Throughout the last decade, open bookcases began to crop up on the streets of Frankfurt. Known locally as *Offener Bücherschrank,* these small weatherproof cabinets provide free access to reading material for all comers. The idea is to bring a book you've read and take one you haven't. Small teams of volunteers oversee their upkeep. On streets such as Bergerstraße and Leipzigerstraße, Gallusanlage and Oeder Weg, these open bookcases are an everyday example of the special place that the written word has in the life of Frankfurt.

COPYRIGHT

OPEN BOOKCASE

Collected Stories

English Creative Writing Group Frankfurt

Copyright © 2018 English Creative Writing Group Frankfurt and with the authors.

All rights reserved. No part of this book may be reproduced in any form or by any electronic or mechanical means, including information storage and retrieval systems, without permission in writing from the publisher.

All stories are copyright of their respective creators as indicated herein, and are reproduced here with permission.

ACKNOWLEDGEMENT

Meet-Up Organiser

Martin Gamble

Editor

Julie Sheridan

Proofreading

Lesley Warren

Layout and Design

Marion Hermannsen

Cover Image & Design

Brian Dilg

Writing Exercise Moderators

Brian Dilg, Lidia Galli, Martin Gamble, Marion Hermannsen, Michael Kasper, Joël Linger, Ilias Nikolaidis, Julie Sheridan

Published by English Creative Writing Group, Frankfurt.

Thanks to all of our families and friends, and to the staff at Le Méridien, Frankfurt for patiently distributing drinks as we furiously scribble and type.

CONTENTS

FOREWORD	ix
ABOUT THE AUTHORS	xiii
A HUSBAND'S CALL TO DUTY	1
A VERY SMART MOVE	3
AFFAIR	7
ALICE	13
ALL THIS STUFF	18
ARISTODEMUS OF SPARTA	22
BIRDS	26
DOC B	30
DREAM OF A LAKE HOUSE	34
GEMS OF A KIND	40
HEATDAYZE	42
IFE	46
IRREVERENCE	48
KNOCK ON ANY DOOR	52
LAUGHTER AT THE LORD OF SILENCE	53
LET LOOSE	57
NOTHING	59
PARKING SUNS	63
PERMIT	67
SALVATION	69
SEASON SEQUINS	73
SECRET	76
SHABBIR	80
SPOON	86
STEP BY STEP	88
STORY OF A PIXEL	92
TEETH	93
THE BRIEF CHRONICLER	96
THE FIRST DAY	99

THE MOONLIGHT ON A THURSDAY	100
THE PLAY	109
THE SONG	113
THE TEST	117
THE UNHAPPY ABACUS	121
TWO DRAFTS	125
WHAT'S THE WORST THAT CAN HAPPEN?	128

FOREWORD
BY MARTIN GAMBLE

When I first moved to Frankfurt two years ago, I decided to start my own writing group, even though I had never done anything like this before. I wanted the group's meetings to be something fun and creative to do on a Sunday morning, with the added benefit of building a network of like-minded friends.

Three people came to the first meeting, then more and more people joined as the weeks went by. We quickly established a familiar routine: introductions and quick word games, followed by the first writing exercise.

The idea of the writing exercises is to help people overcome the fear of a blank page. Most writers could write about a million different topics, but when they come to write that first sentence, it isn't helpful that a million ideas have come to the forefront of their mind all at once.

The exercises provide a little focus to allow the trickle of creative juices to flow. We usually write for twenty minutes, then go around the table to allow each writer to either give a summary of what they have written and share their creative process, or to have a chance to read their story out loud.

This is where the magic happens. We soon learned that

everyone writes wildly differently to each other. Some people write in the first person, some in the second person; some write in the past, others in the present or future; some write romance or horror or comedy or sci-fi or historical stories; some write monologues and some write dialogues.

After working within your own creative universe for these twenty minutes, to then discover the universes of the other writers has endless benefits. It allows us to highlight and define our own style, because when we hear and identify the style of another writer, it reflects both the strengths and weaknesses of both the writing that we're hearing and the writing that we've just finished.

We pick out the little elements that we would never have thought of ourselves, things that are outside of our skill pools. This prompts us to think, to reflect on how we might try to incorporate new elements into our own writing next time.

What I find most beautiful about our group is the way we discuss things. Writers all seem to have a similar temperament, are often visual thinkers and tend to be more introverted. If we were discussing these topics in a corporate environment, they would be loud, fast, aggressive and dominated by extroverts.

In our group, it's different. No matter if someone deeply disagrees with a topic, a line of dialogue, a character's idiosyncrasy or a choice of words, everything is discussed in such a calm, understanding and thought-provoking way. I believe this comes from the writer's innate desire to understand the world in its entirety.

To show one hundred per cent compassion for an opposing opinion is the greatest step a writer can make in understanding a character or a situation or a choice. This understanding has the chance to bubble up to the surface at a later date and spill out onto a page in the form of words in a story.

With the English Creative Writing Group, Frankfurt, I found

something beyond anything I could have ever imagined. We have over eight hundred members, with a core of around fifty regular members. Some come every week, others most weeks, others some weeks, and still others occasionally.

That's the beauty of having such a relaxed and informal group of people looking for something fun to do on a Sunday morning. We mix it up, too, with writing exercises, focused sessions to work on our own projects, motivation/accountability sessions, feedback sessions and workshops.

Just like the most precious element of Frankfurt's city culture, our group is rich in diversity. We have established authors who have already published books, and aspiring writers who are looking for their first opportunity to translate their creative ideas into compelling narratives. Every single person brings something valuable to the table.

Having such a variety of styles cultivates our gratitude for our own individuality, and it was this idea that first gave birth to the idea of an anthology of stories. All the stories in this book were created during or drew inspiration from our Sunday sessions, and each is uniquely different to represent the spectrum of stories written in our meetings.

We are proud to have captured a flavour of our wonderful Sunday morning sessions here for you to read and enjoy.

Frankfurt
October 2018

ABOUT THE AUTHORS

Ilona Ahonen rents a micro-flat next to the European Central Bank and works in the pharmaceutical industry. In her free time, she watches YouTube makeup tutorials, although she hardly ever puts on any makeup. Ilona lived in Frankfurt from 2008 to 2015 and returned in 2017. She originally comes from Finland. With her excellent eyesight and limited hearing ability, Ilona is a better reader than listener and struggles listening to other writers' stories in the writing exercises group. However, in one session she managed to hear the word 'birds', and that is when her story in this Anthology started to evolve.

Anurag seems to be the kid who decided never to grow up. People, places, stories, everything and everyone fascinates him. He is also the most 'Indian' Indian you would meet. He is never on time and always has an opinion about everything. He loves to talk, through words and otherwise, of love and other things.

Krysta Brown is an expatriate American nomad now living outside of Frankfurt, after having previously lived in Leipzig, Hamburg, China and various US cities. She has a background in and passion for journalism but has recently switched sides to test the waters of public relations. Above all, she admires good storytelling in any form and language and still misses the Fourth of July barbecues and wide-open spaces of her home state.

Irina Burkova is from Moscow, Russia. She has lived in Frankfurt since 2012. She works in IT and had never tried creative writing before joining her first English Creative Writing Group meet-up in 2018.

Jenny Burns is a complete novice writer who enjoys watching cities that she has probably only recently moved to.

Justina Dešriūtė is a web developer from Lithuania who enjoys playing with words just as much as with guitar strings. Currently living in Frankfurt, she is rediscovering herself as a storyteller, enjoying each and every Sunday in the Creative Writing Group sharing her tales with the like-minded.

Brian Dilg is an American writer and filmmaker. He's published two books of non-fiction, and has received numerous awards for his screenwriting and cinematography. He started dabbling in fiction in 2017. As a young child, his babysitters demanded that his mother tell them the secret of how she managed to train him to sit quietly and read books all day. She modestly claimed that he just always liked books. Not much has changed.

Lidia Galli was born in Italy, but her need to travel led her to Japan and Germany, places she now considers her *home sweet home* as much as Italy. A heavy tea drinker and reading addict, she loves any kind of book she can get her hands on. Born with a love for writing, Lidia tries very hard to improve her writing skills, despite life leaving her few moments alone with her pen.

Martin Gamble is a Yorkshire man living in Frankfurt and is the founding member of the English Creative Writing Group, Frankfurt. He grew up in Barwick-in-Elmet, a small village in Leeds famous for its Maypole celebrations. During the past twenty years, he has worked on a variety of project management roles that focus on branding and marketing. In 2014, he completed a BA Hons degree in Creative Writing, fulfilling his teenage desire to become a writer. Martin says, 'I love our writing network in Frankfurt. Working with other aspiring writers is a creative nexus of energy that helps me translate my wild imagination and write unique and entertaining stories.'

Sven Hinrichs was born in 1964. Black and white photographs prove his early excitement in reading out stories to his younger sister. It did not disturb him at all, nor anybody else, that he held magazines like *Stern* upside down. As time went by, his reading material broadened from various comics to books like *Last Man on Earth*. Obligatory literature was read, but almost immediately forgotten. Studies in Sven's third decade allowed him to find out about the senselessness of scientific investigations in and on language in depth. *Four Master Tropes* marked this climax. He has since increased his efforts to replace reading with writing. *Laughter at the Lord of Silence* is one of these attempts.

Marion Hermannsen writes Urban Fantasy as Ella J. Smyth and Gay Romance as EJ Smyth. She draws her inspiration from real life, but makes it so much better by adding copious amounts of magic and romance. Marion loves to combine her German and Irish backgrounds to create new and unique stories. Myths and fairy tales from all over the world are of particular interest to her, although she adapts them to fit her imagination. A happy ending is (nearly) always guaranteed!

Nino Khundadze was born in Tbilisi, Georgia, during the Soviet Union, witnessing its end as a child. She was totally into art from early childhood. She trained as an architect and worked for several years. After this, her life changed, transformed from the usual one into something totally different, full of adventures, full of stories that one might not even believe were real. Life brought her back to art. The impressions and experiences she gained from it all made her start writing again. So, here she is, sharing the world through her eyes with her art and writings.

Martina Lackner is German-Austrian and lives in Frankfurt. She lived and studied for four years in Austria and the Netherlands. Martina is trained in Healthcare Policy, Innovation and Management and works in Business Planning and Strategy for a pharmaceutical service provider. Martina began to write in her free time when she was sixteen: from diary writing to poems and philosophical pieces. Recently, she has also started to write short stories. Martina is passionate about travelling, discussing politics – especially feminism – and enjoying herself in nature.

Christopher Morahan moved to Frankfurt from Dublin in July 2017, and was very lucky to discover the English Creative Writing Group soon thereafter. On those odd Sunday mornings when he is not excessively hungover, he loves coming to Le Méridien to write stories that would take him much longer to conceive if he was simply procrastinating at his desk in Bornheim. This particular story was inspired by a production of *Hamlet* which he saw with his father in London in August 2017. As is the case with everything else that Christopher has written since he came to Frankfurt, writing this story would not have been possible were it not for the energy and encouragement of his fellow group members.

Ilias Nikolaidis is a Doctor in Engineering who finds it amusing referring to himself in the third person. Until a year ago, his contribution to fiction consisted of numerous technical reports, which were all loosely based on true facts. Since then, he has been trying to make as many blunders as possible in order to improve his writing style. He is a firm believer in 'learning by failing.' He lives according to what he preaches, which explains why he is still single.

Ekaterina Novgorodtseva writes short stories in her spare time in genres ranging from humour to horror, fantasy to sci-fi, and everything in between. She is a student of Business Informatics at Goethe University in Frankfurt.

Yousif Shamsa is an engineer who recently discovered a new passion for writing thanks to the English Creative Writing Group. Originally from Iraq, Yousif currently lives in the Netherlands.

Julie Sheridan is from Ireland. A lot of her stories are set in pubs. She is trying to work out if this is a coincidence. She writes short stories, flash fiction and poems and is in the process of writing a novel for children. She finds it a challenge to write without using the 'bad F word'.

Ian Stout grew up reading young adult fiction like the *Percy Jackson* and *Harry Potter* series. He was born in Santa Cruz, California on a Monday, and believes that all days of the week are created equal. He spends his free time writing and travelling to places he's never been to before.

Erika Surat Andersen is originally from the San Francisco Bay Area and loves storytelling in all its forms. She's a filmmaker, screenwriter and university lecturer in the Frankfurt area. Before moving to Germany, she was a professor in film and television at Loyola Marymount University in Los Angeles for several years. Erika still misses the Pacific Ocean, but the rivers and bike paths in Frankfurt are great and her family definitely keeps her on her toes. Erika mightily enjoys creative writing and sharing stories with others.

Elena Viso is the type of friend that everyone has – the one that always ruins the food, even a simple sandwich – and is super lazy but, somehow, ends up having ridiculous unplanned adventures. The best part about reading and writing is that you can be both – lazy and having an adventure – at the same time. Efficiency!

Karen Vuong was born in Los Angeles, California. While pursuing a career as an opera singer, she has also lived in New York, New Jersey, and Frankfurt. Creative writing is a new passion for her, and she is thrilled to be able to add it to the ever-growing list of hobbies intended to keep her out of trouble. Her entry in this Anthology is dedicated to her fiancé, Ryan, and their cat, Ichabod.

Lesley Warren was made in the UK, but contains some foreign parts. She is a lifelong linguist, a reformed perfectionist and is constantly dressing wrongly for the weather. She would like to actually finish writing a novel one day, but consoles herself with the thought that existence itself can be an art form. She may have to settle for that.

A HUSBAND'S CALL TO DUTY

BY KAREN VUONG

I love my wife. She's supportive, kind, gentle, sexy, smart, funny, and she is eight months pregnant with our first child. I can already see her yelling at the referee for a bad call at our future kid's Little League game. She'll be a great mom. I LOVE MY WIFE.

It's the dead of night when I feel a nudge in my back from the ballooning stomach of my better half.

'Babe?' she whispers.

I DO NOT LOVE being woken up in the middle of the night, but I love my wife.

'Yeah?'

'We...' (she only speaks in the plural since she found out we had a bun in the oven) '...need fried chicken... please.'

'Sweetheart, it's two a.m.' I yawn to make a point.

'I know, I know, but it's not ME that wants it... It's the baby. Don't you want your baby to form properly? You wouldn't build a house with the wrong materials, would you??'

I groggily get up. 'Where am I supposed to get fried chicken this late??'

'WE don't have any idea, but we know you'll figure it out,

because future Dad is the best. We love you!' They blow me a kiss.

Smiling, my wife (and boulder) rolls over, places her iPad mini on her stomach and proceeds to watch Netflix, waiting expectantly.

An image of a *Best Dad-to-Be* trophy held overhead flashes in my mind. I'm a man. Hell, I'm a DAD. I can provide for my family. I can totally do this. I hunker down at the edge of the bed to check Google for ten minutes. There is no late-night delivery. And the roads are so iced over, I don't want to risk denying my kid of a dad all for a late-night craving run.

I head downstairs to the kitchen. This isn't the first fried chicken craving. There must be some leftovers in the fridge, anything just to scratch that itch. The cold air blows against my face, illuminated by the glow of the fridge light. Nothing.

I open the freezer, praying for some miracle. The chilly taste of plastic and ice enclosed in darkness makes me shiver. Nothing but organic mint ice cream and frozen fruit. Damn.

I need to take a moment to collect my thoughts. I pull on my rubber boots and heavy jacket, and head to the backyard. The moon lights up the snow, silhouetting the bare trees filled with chubby pigeons nestled together for warmth. There is an expectant quiet. Slowly fading into my aural vision, I hear coos coming from my neighbours' yard. I look over the fence and see their chicken coop.

Leaning against a tree is a pair of pruning shears, the moonlight gleaming wickedly off the blades. I look back and forth between the trees and the coop. I love my wife.

A VERY SMART MOVE

BY IRINA BURKOVA

'Is this one of those times when you want me to lie to protect your delicate emotions?' Celia is as direct as ever, a quality I usually appreciate in my friends. Not today, though.

'No, please be your usual self and spit out the bitter truth to me. Is this thing really standing out?'

I have been staring at my reflection in the corridor mirror for the better part of half an hour. My face is heavily bruised and even a two centimetre-thick layer of makeup can't really hide it. I've spent no less than two hours watching YouTube tutorials on disguise makeup. On top of that, there is a band-aid on my forehead, failing to hide a huge scratch. It's not really the right look for a fashion TV reporter. Well, for a first-day-on-the-dream-job fashion TV reporter.

'Honey, it does *not* stand out. Perhaps, people will think you have some congenital disease which gives your skin this charming blueish colour.' Celia is not only direct, but also pretty damn rude.

'Even so, it's probably better that way. The most important thing is that they don't know the truth. I don't think my boss will be too keen on keeping me after the probation period if he finds out that I'm not smart enough to go to a bowling alley without humiliating myself and landing on my face on a bowling lane.'

'It just proves you are the PERFECT fit for the job! Looks and fashion are everything and proper bowling shoes are ugly and useless.' Celia giggles and I know she is right – it was not smart to play in an absolutely beautiful but slippery pair of pumps. I take a deep breath and, fully determined, turn away from the mirror.

'No preaching, please. I need to go, I don't want to add unpunctuality to my list of sins. Not today. Wish me luck, Celia!' I shiver just a little bit when she hugs me. My ribs hurt almost as much as my face.

'Break a leg, honey!'

By the time I arrive at this fancy club, the cameraman, Hugo, has everything set up. He's got a very good spot, right next to the red carpet, so we can be the first ones to catch Jasmine when she arrives. Fabulous, incomparable Jasmine, the celebrity with an impeccable reputation. I've heard that Hugo is extremely professional and they often pair him up with the newbies. However, today, I am not sure that even Hugo's expertise can save the situation. Maybe he can switch on some magical filters. And it is almost completely dark in here too, after all. Hugo studies me slowly from head to toe but does not give away any sign of surprise, expect maybe his left eyebrow, which he raises just a tiny bit too high.

'There you are! At least you're not late.'

'Hugo, listen, I know it looks as if...'

He breaks me off and says 'Tacenda...'

I have no idea what he means. It sounds like Latin – this guy is Portuguese, after all. But I don't dare to ask and, luckily, he does not give me time to do so.

'Move a bit to the left, yes, here.'

Before I get too nervous, repeating the prepared questions in my head for a thousandth time, she appears. Elegant silver dress, all in sequins, glowing skin, beautifully styled hair. Gorgeous, as I always imagined when watching such reportages on my parents' couch before. And now I am in one of them myself. I am actually conducting one! The crowd begins to shout and wave and I am blinded for a second by the camera flashes from all directions. But it is now or never. I take a step forward.

'Jasmine, Ashbourne Fashion TV here. We are extremely happy to welcome you to town today! How do you like Ashbourne?'

It's a miracle she hears me. She looks like a queen and she behaves like one too. As far as I can judge as I've never seen a real queen before.

'Delighted to be here and thank you for such a sweet welcome! Aaahm...' She falls silent for a second and carefully studies my face. I am not sure whether I should shoot another question or wait until she continues.

'I am really impressed with the level of social responsibility in your town and the inclusivity you exercise here. More towns in America should follow your path. It will be an honour for me to share this experience with others, wherever I go. All the best to you, darling!' She looks at me one last time with some signs of pity in her eyes and, before I can open my mouth again, she is already smiling at the competitor's camera.

Inclusivity? What the hell? My questions on her favourite interior designers and yoga practices don't fit at all after her inclusivity reference, so it might be just as well that she turned away before I could demonstrate my total lack of professionalism with thirty seconds of awkward silence live on air.

Everything happened so fast. I still could not digest it, while Hugo was already packing up all of his equipment.

'I am so sorry, Hugo, I... em... could not grasp her attention for long enough.'

Hugo does not seem to care and is obviously not generally a very talkative guy. I retreat to my smartphone and start scrolling frantically through my messages. The variety of texts goes from my mom's *Your first live broadcast, sweetie, so proud of you!!* to... No! Wait a second. There is *already* a message from my boss. Don't panic, don't panic, what is the worst thing that can actually happen?

Miss Grant, I am very sorry to find out that you suffer from such a rare disease, as Miss Jasmine has pointed out, and I am also very grateful that you did not bring it up at our interviews, to make sure we take an unbiased decision when recruiting you. It was definitely very brave of you to show it today and also a very smart move for a reporter in terms of timing. We all know that Jasmine is a huge supporter of medical research in general, and is donating very generously to our local hospital. Her words today give very good publicity. Thank you for the work you've done.

I am numb. What is he talking about?! I start Googling Jasmine and all these pictures come up: Jasmine with the mayor, Jasmine in the hospital, Jasmine in the hospital with a group of kids, Jasmine in the hospital with the group of kids with suspiciously blueish skin...

And then Celia's phrase pierces through my mind: *congenital disease*. So, wait, do I look a little bit like...? Did she think that I'm...?

Great. Well done, Katie! This blueish bruised face is now your trademark. What a start to my career. I'll need to get a bowling membership card and I'll need it fast!

AFFAIR

BY ANURAG

He looks at his key card. There are some signs and symbols here and there, but they are not important. His eyes are fixed on the words *Valid only during your stay*. Why would they mention something like that? It is not like he is going to stay beyond his *stay*. What if he does? Just to prove a point? What if he stayed forever in this hotel room, 'til the day he couldn't live anymore, and they would have to carry his perished carcass out of the room?

The housekeeping will be questioned about what kind of person he was. The receptionist, who always wears red lipstick and a very tight skirt, will act nervous throughout the proceedings, maybe leading the cops into suspicion about her involvement in his demise. Even though it would neither be a murder nor a suicide, cops would suspect and investigate. That's what cops do. They investigate and waste their time over the most trivial matters. But they get paid for it. He gets paid for bringing business to his company – attending meetings, finding clients, luring them into the dreamland that his company promises to be. He is also responsible for paying the cops to keep their mouths shut, to *cooperate*. It is a part of the deal. He is a businessman.

If he stays forever in this hotel room, will his company reimburse his stay? What if they fire him? The HR people are conniving in that sense. They would rather let a person go instead of fulfilling his hotel room fantasies. He is only likeable while he is financially feasible. What would his wife and son back home think?

He is forty-five, his wife a year older. It was a love marriage. He wished he had a daughter, but he doesn't complain about the son either. If he never returns, most definitely his wife would conclude that he was having an affair. An affair in a European city. Most probably with a European woman. Maybe Romanian. They are easy, he hears. His wife would lodge a complaint with the cops, maybe file for divorce. Things can go haywire very quickly, you see.

Women are presumptuous. They don't seek evidence before convicting someone. But also, women are such an important creation of God. Such a beautiful piece of work. If, let's say, he had to have an affair, and if he was to stay in the hotel room forever and if he was to have a divorce with his wife anyway, he would rather have an affair with the receptionist who wears red lipstick and tight skirts. She is very attractive, and it will be convenient. She must just press some buttons in the elevator and knock on his door. Anything but this brumous life would do. But that's too far-fetched, he realises. A woman as good-looking as her would not be interested in a man with a balding head and bulging belly who decided to stay in a hotel room all his life. She is also a woman. She would want a young, virile man, who would promise her a future and kids and would rather buy her a mansion.

Hotel rooms are not romantic. A nice getaway for a day or

two maybe, but forever? He has never heard of anyone doing that.

What will the world think? More so of him staying permanently in the hotel room than his affair? Affairs are a common thing. But a man who decided to spend all his life in a hotel room just to test a key card? He should be put into an asylum.

He switches on the TV and puts on some news channel. He could see the news headlines printed all over the media, news anchors debating over his choice. Maybe they would bring his wife and children on TV. Maybe the divorce filing would be a live event covered across the world. BBC, CNN, Fox, Guardian. All cameras on his wife's hands, while she signs her side of the deal. That might be ugly.

He switches off the TV. It's too unsettling. He needs to feel better about himself. After spending almost all your life without a purpose, after losing all your time while gaining all your weight, the only good thing about life is an outrageous dream, an unlikely adventure. Like an affair with the receptionist. She is hot. See? He is doing it again. This is what he does. He doesn't even have to close his eyes.

Anyway, right now he is feeling low and lonely. He reminds himself of his wife. How much he loves her. Of course he does. But he needs to feel it. He needs to feel the love towards his wife. It must be done right now.

He connects his phone to his laptop with a data cable. Their last trip to Kathmandu is all captured in these photographs. He realises how fat his wife has become. Fat and old. In a way, they look like two sides of the same entity. The diameters of their bellies, if measured, might turn out to be the exact same. Even their faces have started to look like each other. As if they were siblings. Both wearing glasses on their curiously small eyes. He doesn't feel any love. Instead he becomes sad. He simply scrolls through the images.

There are some pictures of the landscape. His son is turning into a fine photographer. Maybe he will send him to NYU for a degree in photography. There must be such a course. But before deciding for him, he would ask the boy's wish too. He is not an authoritarian father. He sighs. He could have been something else if his father had asked his wish before sending him to study law. Then, almost out of compulsion, he had to get into management. One can't simply earn enough with a law degree. Corruption is the first and foremost rule. You must be corrupt and ready to give in to the system. He has done it one better. He has started loving the system. But he doesn't love his wife. Wait. No. He didn't say that. He can't say that. It is his only medal of self-esteem. He got to marry the woman he loved. But now she looks like his sibling. Maybe spending so many years with a person causes hormonal changes. Maybe he should have taken biology as his major. Maybe he would be a better doctor. Who knows? But he knows that he still loves his wife. He definitely loves her. He is pretty sure about it.

He realises that it's about the time that the receptionist would finish her shift and go home. He gets up from the bed, looks in the mirror and shuts the door behind him.

The elevator hits the ground floor. The doors part. The light from within the elevator has created a spectrum in the dim-lit hallway. A slender figure is walking through this spectrum as he is about to get out. The slender figure turns out to be the receptionist. She is wearing her red lipstick and tight skirt.

He has been dreaming of this moment all his stay. They are alone. He feels a sensation. A tingle of excitement. What to do next? She is half his age. He doesn't want to leave a bad impression. What if he says something inappropriate and she just storms off? Is the elevator even moving? He looks at the buttons. One for the fan, one for the light. Then there are buttons for each floor from 0 till 21. There is also -1. That's where his car would be parked if he had to stay here forever. -1 is what the receptionist has pressed. It seems she owns a car. Good for her. At such a young age. It's commendable. It's also hot.

It is also hot outside. Summer in Europe can be absolutely nightmarish. How long does it take to get from 0 to -1? It's crazy. Something must be done. He is pretty sure the elevator is stuck in infinity or some other loop of time.

'So, what happens if I press this button?' he asks, looking at a button with a fake phone printed on it. 'Does it even work?'

The receptionist first makes sure that he is talking to her. Before his question, he was invisible to her, almost fictional. But now he exists. She is still in the hotel premises, a staff member. He is a customer. Customers can be creepy, but they are gods nevertheless. It is in the manual. She must pout and say something fake and supportive or at least nod. She goes with the nod.

'Yes, sir. It most certainly does, I guess.'

He wants to test her word. He is a little freaked out right now, so the button better work. He pushes it. Not with one but with two fingers. There is a light out and a little quake within the elevator.

'Actually, it's when you let go of that button that things get nasty.'

He hears, in the dark, the receptionist laugh out loud. Her laughter fills up the entire space in the elevator. There is hardly any space left for him to stand. There is darkness and laughter. Soon, he is gasping for air and light.

THUD!

The elevator crashes against some ground. Suddenly there is a blinding light, as if he has landed straight on the sun. He is burning, he feels vertigo hitting him. He opens his eyes. There is a woman staring at him with fear, almost identical to himself.

'Are you okay?'

He looks around. The curtains have been pulled aside. It's

not the hotel room; just his normal bedroom. The bedsheet is crumpled beside him. He didn't sleep alone. Did he sleep with the receptionist? This woman is not the receptionist. Who is this woman?

'Who are you, woman?' he is just about to ask when he recognises her. It's his wife. Of course, it is his wife. Thank God it is his wife.

'What happened? she asks, worried.

'Nothing. Nothing.'

She mumbles something to herself. She looks different from the pictures of Kathmandu, different from him. As different as a woman looks from a man.

'You look beautiful,' he says in a stroke of self-realisation.

She just gives him that look. That pseudo-angry look she always gives when she is buying his words. It has been a while since the two of them touched each other on purpose. This is his first attempt at flirting in about a month.

'How about I take a day off today? I don't feel like leaving you alone,' he murmurs.

She lets a smile pass over her face. She decides that it's the moisturiser. These anti-ageing things really work. Or maybe it is the dream he was into. He was sweating. Whatever he did in there. She doesn't want to know. She doesn't mind either.

ALICE

BY BRIAN DILG

The sun is hot on her neck. The cobblestones are old. This is a guess. Does she know anything about cobblestones? They're saddened with rain.

It must be a European city. Has she been to Europe? This is another question. The rain has the answers.

There's a café. She decides to order coffee. The waiter has only one arm. His black apron is stained with white.

This matters. She can't say why.

She doesn't understand his words. She says something she hopes is *coffee, please*. He nods. He understands her. She doesn't understand herself.

A woman strides by wearing a long skirt. It's bold red, slit high. She wishes she could walk like this woman, confident her legs looked great. Her name is Alice.

Is Alice the woman in the red skirt? She might be excused from knowing the woman's name, but she should know her own. She waits for words to enlighten her. She peers at her own legs. Are they hers?

The waiter brings a white cup filled with black liquid. Steam curls over the rim. The word *porcelain* appears. She can't remember anyone saying it. Has the cup explained itself? Does it want to be introduced?

She sniffs it. Animals sniff when they want to know more. Some animals kill other animals. Is she that kind of animal?

She sips cautiously. She has experience with hot liquids. It burns her tongue. Perhaps she has no experience after all. Is it coffee? She tastes nothing. She can't remember how coffee tastes. It might be motor oil. She grips the arms of her chair, suddenly blinded by a fear of being crushed.

A bell rings. It appears to be a large bell. 'Appears' means how things *look*, not how things *are*.

Everything appeared fine.

Someone is narrating. Does she know more than Alice? Does *she* have a family? Were things fine for this she who might be Alice?

She can't drink it. She's developed a new reflex: *don't drink coffee*. She doesn't know if it *is* coffee, but it's singed her. She isn't going to be lured by it again. She has experience. It's made her giddy.

There's a spire. Does the church know her? That isn't the question. Does she know anyone? She knows the waiter, but she doesn't understand him. She knows the dark puddles between the cobblestones. They reflect nothing. They ignore the blue sky. They've judged her. They won't say why.

This bell is going to tell her everything.

She'd been a stranger to herself, but that's over.

She doesn't want to know.

She's falling through thunderclouds at terrifying speed. Her arms stretch out as if the clouds could stop her. There's a faint bell. Two, then three. Perhaps a dozen. They clank awkwardly. They aren't church bells. There's a confused thunder. She breaks through the clouds.

It isn't thunder.

Cows are running down a steep hill. They've been spooked.

They might be chasing each other because they're young. Young things play. She too had played once because she was young and had no idea what awaited her.

The cows would stop where the pasture flattened, and she'd land on them. When cows are scared, they're stupid. She doesn't want the cows to get hurt. Why has she been so stupid?

She regrets her shoes. They're a dangerous red. Who wears red spike heels to a pasture? This isn't where she'd been going. The cows keep running. There's a gate in the fence. Someone's left it open.

She has a terrible feeling: she was thirteen. Their golden retriever Winston hadn't come home the previous night. She'd left the gate open. Her father was furious. She woke up early to search for him. Someone had shot him in the head and left him in the front yard. A message. It's that feeling: it was her fault. She deserved it.

She falls through the sun. It shudders and flees her touch.

There'd been rain on the road. It was after midnight. She should have had the headlight repaired. She'd worn the red dress that showed off her legs. It was the only outfit that could catch Frank's interest. It was pointless. All they did was fight anyway. It was too sexy for Thanksgiving. Looking good in front of his parents was trouble. It would contradict his version of her.

The road was fogged with clouds. She'd looked down at the cigarette lighter for just a moment. She didn't see the first cow until the big sedan rounded the corner. It was an accident.

Wasn't it?

It was Alice who slammed on the brakes, Alice who twisted the wheel. She remembers with shame feeling thankful that the car skidded to the right because her husband's side would strike the cow standing in the road. It was looking up at them, its huge, soft eyes confused in the headlights.

Frank had thrown his arm in front of his face. The cow crashed through the window. It sheared off his arm like butter. His arm struck her face, slapping her one last time even as it left his body. His parents hated her. They couldn't suspect *him* of anything unseemly. It might implicate them as parents. She'd told him that she'd drop him at the top of the driveway. She'd drive the four hours home alone. She'd pack her things and disappear before he could find her and hit her again.

She should have just stayed in her pen. That's what good cows did. It was his favourite nickname for her: *you fucking cow*. Did you say 'nickname' for names that weren't sweet?

The bell rings and rings. There's a church outside the hospital window. The sun hurts her eyes. She wishes the nurse would shut the blinds.

There's a white teacup and a red pack of Marlboros next to her bed, unopened. Her brand.

She manages to knock them to the floor.

Her name is Alice.

Finally, the bell stops ringing.

ALL THIS STUFF

BY JULIE SHERIDAN

Blood spilled everywhere. It ran between her fingers, to the sharp corners of her wrists, dropping into a claret puddle on the scrubbed white tiles of the bathroom floor. One hour of yesterday she'd spent on hands and knees, rubber gloves and *Cillit Bang,* scouring that floor until her arms ached. Cursing between clenched teeth with each thrust of the scrubbing brush. What a waste of time.

    She grabbed one cotton wool pad after another, placing them on her violently slashed skin. How quickly they turned from white to red like the petals of a flowering hibiscus in the garden. It was oddly captivating. There had been some hibiscus in that bouquet he'd presented to her ten days ago. Beautifully, rustically wrapped and tied with a rough jute bow. Tasteful. Bespoke. It was a nice surprise, granted. Marjorie couldn't remember the last time he'd bought her flowers. But a bouquet this elegant could not have been selected by a man, least of all *her* man. A dozen red roses were about as far as Jerome's thoughtfulness would stretch and if he paid attention at all he would have known that she hated red roses. Ghastly. The last vestige of the table-to-table seller in a tourist restaurant. It was a measly, snivelling criticism she'd tried to bat away when she saw how shyly he had proffered the flowers. Twenty-two years of marriage and he was still worried what she might think of him. It would have been heart-melting if it wasn't so fucking irritating. God, another negative thought. Could the poor bastard do anything right?

'Take a lover,' her friend Vanessa had said when she'd first intimated that all was not a bed of roses with Jerome. They were having lunch at the gallery and the second bottle of rosé had unhitched Marjorie's usual circumspection. She'd laughed so heartily that wine had gushed out of her nostrils, but became quite flustered when she sensed other diners looking disapprovingly at her, noting the empty bottle of wine beside the one just opened on the table.

'Fuck *them*,' Vanessa had hissed, sloshing wine onto the white linen tablecloth as she pointed in a circular motion. 'Puckered as pugs' anuses. Might as well be dead for the amount of life left in them.'

It was easy for Vanessa. She'd chosen her role a long time ago. Flirting and giggling and being amenable to those who were charmed by her, waving two fingers at those who weren't. She was happy to be bankrolled by Tim the Tosser but happier still to take up with whichever tennis coach or handyman took her fancy. It would be amusing if it wasn't so tragically clichéd. The lack of romance involved in infidelity was what Marjorie found utterly unappealing. The sordidness, the duplicity, the sneaking about were all anathema to her. But it was the gruesome reality of spurting bodily fluids and rapacious grunting and unfortunately sprouting hairs that bothered her more. An uncomfortable hour with a marriage counsellor was nothing by comparison to all of that grubbiness.

'Make more of an effort,' Gail the counsellor had told Jerome gently before they left their one and only appointment.

'And *you* need to be more forgiving,' she'd said to Marjorie, pointedly arching an eyebrow as she ushered them out of her warm office into the stark coldness of the corridor outside. They'd held hands then, just briefly, as she walked him to the train station. 'I need to get back to work,' Jerome had said, glancing at his watch, 'but we'll talk about all this *stuff* later.' By the time he'd returned from work that evening, Marjorie was asleep, tucked neatly over her side of the bed, a vast continent of exasperation between her pillow and his. They never had talked about 'all this stuff.' The bouquet, and now the opera tickets, were his way of showing he was making more of an effort.

✦

Jerome banged on the bathroom door. He hated being late. Two hundred and twenty pounds on tickets for the opera and Marjorie was dawdling as usual. He could feel his blood pressure creeping skywards with every passing second. Fourteen-hour days at work were never this stressful. He could manage a staff of two hundred, artfully ironing out any creases that threatened the stability of the firm. Anticipating difficulties, reacting appropriately, motivating and incentivising; it all came so readily to him. Why, then, was dealing with this woman so infuriatingly stressful?

'Don't come in,' she screeched from the other side of the door when he pushed down on the handle. She sounded deranged.

'We need to leave in five minutes, Marjorie,' he said, deliberately officious. The reply from the bathroom sounded feral, a strangely high-pitched growl. Jerome got down on all fours and lowered his cheek to the floor. Through the gap between the bottom of the door and the floor beneath it, he caught sight of a pool of red. *Christ,* he thought as his stomach lurched and his mind began to sprint to all sorts of new places. He knew she'd been a bit testy of late, teary even, but he wouldn't have said *depressed*. And he certainly wouldn't have considered her *suicidal*. He took a deep breath, pushed down on the handle and shouldered the door open.

'I told you not to come in,' Marjorie whispered. She was hunkered down and surrounded by bloodied cotton wool. Jerome bent low beside her, lifting her gently to sit on the edge of the bath. 'Here, let me get something for *that*,' he said, fishing out a sterile dressing from the cabinet. He held a facecloth to her leg until the bleeding stopped and then covered it with a bandage. As leg-shaving accidents went, it was pretty dramatic.

'I was trying to make more of an effort,' she said, laughing as he carried her to the sofa.

'Fuck making an effort,' he said, ripping up the opera tickets.

ARISTODEMUS OF SPARTA
BY ILIAS NIKOLAIDIS

He stands next to me. Covered in metal and muscles and scars.

He is big. I mean, of course he is. But, even amongst the Spartans, he sure is a big one.

I do not know why he ended up standing next to me in the phalanx. Usually the position next to the *amateurs,* as they enjoy calling us, is reserved for the weakest of them. No opportunity missed by the Spartans to remind us of their contempt. It's not as if they try to keep it a secret.

Maybe he did something to piss off their second king, after Leonidas fell in Thermopylae.

He stands at attention. Still.

Still as the cord of a curved bow, fully drawn and craving to release death upon anyone willing to contest him. He looks like he is about to snap at the slightest provocation.

My shield looks pitiful and way too colourful next to his. A wooden construction covered with layers of thick bleached hide, painted with the bright colours of my neighbourhood and having something approximating an owl drawn on it. Truth be told, four out of five people need to be told what it is before they recognise it.

His, on the contrary, is a plain slab of polished bronze. Identical for every Spartan, decorated only with the letter *lambda*. Lakedaimonios. He of Lakonia, the land Spartans call their own. As if anyone would need to be reminded which land gives birth to these killers of men.

I force myself to breathe. I know that my duty is to keep his right side covered. Keep the phalanx intact. Hold the line. The signal is given and we start marching forwards, to meet three times as many Persians.

The battle is finally over. My Corinthian-style helmet, inherited from an older cousin crippled in Marathon, is lying on the plains of Plataea and so am I. I try to keep my arms from shaking. I am not sure if it is from the exhaustion or from the cold. Despite being drenched in sweat, despite the hot summer day, it feels like someone has poured ice into my veins. I tap the helmet to praise it for protecting me. It replies with the dull sound of a cracked bowl, telling me that its days of service to my family line are over. There is a deep scratch starting very close to one of the eye sockets, courtesy of a Persian spear. I have been lucky. I'll have to make a gift to Athena as soon as I'm back for keeping me safe.

Maybe I should gift something to Ares as well. Clearly it was he that was fighting next to me, not a Spartan. He was cutting down anyone that stood in front of us. And not with the trained manner which has made Spartans the envy and terror of any General. No. Ares had clearly taken over him. Gone were the control and method of the most effective, dispassionate killing machine of all the Greeks, replaced by the fury and bloodlust and frenzy of the God of War himself. Where I would use my spear to distract the enemy formation, he would thrust deep and true, exposing himself in the process, showing no regard for self-preservation. His spear eventually broke, having laid waste to so many Persians. I thought Ares would leave him then and go possess someone else. But the son of Zeus was clearly having too much fun with this one mortal. So, instead, he made him pull out his spatha with his now bloodied right hand, and urged him to fall upon the Persians with renewed fury.

He rushed into the middle of them like a wild boar on farmers, maiming what was in front of him and around him. I think that was the first time I heard anyone shout and cry at the same time.

He left the safety of our line and charged into the mass of Persians. For a second, I felt the tug of Ares myself, urging me to join him, tempting me with promises of glory and honour. But I could not follow him. The next person had already filled the gap left behind. I wish I could say that it was my duty to the integrity of the phalanx which kept me back, or my protector Athena lending me her wisdom. But the truth of the matter was that I was too scared to do so.

He still lasted longer than any mortal could. Surrounded by enemies, he was generously handing souls to Hermes all around him. It took three blows, each one of which would have stopped any man, to halt his charge. And although he was by that point struck like a sea beast, harpoons sticking out of its hide, he still dealt death to anyone within his reach.

When he eventually went down there was a pile of broken bodies around him. None seemed glad he was gone, Greek or Persian, fearing that Ares might now possess another.

Both sides looked in awe and shock at the mass of broken warriors around them, a testament to his strength and bravery and the violence which binds men together. An offering to the God of War. A pile of flesh, capped with a single battered oversized bronze coin bearing a *lambda*. That should be toll enough for the boatloads crossing Acheron because of him. That should be blood enough to quench even the thirst of Ares himself.

I get up and try to catch my breath. I walk towards the Spartans and ask one of them, pointing towards their lone dead countryman, lying in the centre of the only kind of shrine Ares needs, 'Who was he?'

'He? His name was Aristodemus. He was a coward.'

BIRDS

BY ILONA AHONEN

In spite of their massive size, the flying creatures were such an integral part of the scenery that the villagers never thought about them. Even in ancient drawings, these birds were never illustrated in detail: simple as the earth, obvious as the sky, they never raised further thoughts in the villagers' heads. Until one day, one was found on the ground, dead.

The news was broken by a hunter from the outskirts of the village who, like everybody, had never seen these birds from up close before. The village elder soon sent word for a priest, one of the few who bothered to visit this distant place.

The priest was irritated as he arrived. This would delay his usual work, and he was troubled by the situation of his mother, whose excellent health had rapidly deteriorated without any obvious reason. The village elder walked him to a sturdy carriage where the hunter who had found the corpse was waiting. The hunter would serve as the priest's guide, and the shaken look on his face made the priest increasingly uncomfortable.

'There is an explanation,' the priest told the hunter as the carriage started moving. 'There always is.'

Usually there was nothing supernatural involved: God's ways were mysterious, but His ways were learnt in the realm of everyday things, and the priest mostly ignored old folks' tales of ill omens and did not encourage his people to believe in them. The hunter nodded and looked away.

It was surprisingly easy to walk in the woods that covered the mountain's lower slopes. Following the hunter, the priest finally saw the creature's massive presence looming in the dim forest. The trees were not growing as densely here, and a few of them had fallen. The giant bird that had caused this lay on the ground, legs bent in an awkward position but with an air of gracefulness about it that was not typical for a wild animal. The priest walked around the bird until he reached its head and shuddered as he saw that its eyes were open.

Under its emotionless, unblinking gaze the priest did not feel like the bird was dead, but he knew it was. Even the thought of burying it crossed the priest's mind briefly, but something stopped him from suggesting it: burying seemed too commonplace for these mysterious beings. The feather-covered corpse also seemed disturbingly intact, but maybe it was just the cold air that kept it from rotting.

'Let's leave it here. Let nature work its way,' he said.

Next day, the priest avoided the looks of the villagers who clearly expected something from him. His thoughts wandered from the birds to his sick mother, his town and memories of his youth, things he had not remembered for a long time. Startled, he abruptly realised that he was looking at one of the birds. High in the sky, there was a flying beast so large it should have captured his attention immediately. Yet it fit the scenery so naturally that he had not spotted it.

They must come from the mountains, the priest thought. *Only the mountains are their match.*

He asked for the village elder's carriage again, and the elder nodded without questions. As he was about to leave, the elder handed him a message from his hometown. Feeling suddenly fragile, the priest took the message and left.

His mind numb, the priest read that his mother had drawn her last breath. Several similar cases of illness had emerged now, and the town's physicians were helpless. For a while, the priest wanted to hide in the forest, lie lifeless on the ground like the dead body of the mighty bird. However, the memory of the other bird he had seen flying on the sky came clear to his mind, and after praying for his mother's soul and the life of the others who were ill, the priest started off again.

He travelled the forest path, slowly ascending the mountainside. He drew the air in his lungs, so fresh that he felt like fainting: unlike the villagers, he had not been used to it since birth. Moving higher, the air changed and the priest found himself riding the carriage in a mist, seeing less and less of the road that had become narrower and filled with sharp-edged stones. Descending from the carriage, the priest set the elder's tough little horse free and continued on foot.

The mountain seemed to grow higher and higher the further the priest climbed. Maybe it was his uneasy mind playing tricks, or even a wish of his heart, but he had an eerie feeling of being guided by a force that was greater than him and even greater than the enigmatic birds. The mist was like a waterfall: behind it there was something that was not part of their world, planet, whatever it should be called. He kept climbing the road that was merely a path now and finally reached a small, natural-looking platform at the edge of the mountain. He knew what he would see in the air below it, and there they were: ten, twenty, a hundred, maybe more, all of them majestic, breathtaking, with wingspans longer than any of the trees growing in the forest below. The choice was there, his destiny thrown at him, and he did not hesitate. The priest dropped himself from the platform into the back of the nearest bird and grabbed its feathers. Panting, he squeezed the feathers with all his strength, but the bird did not seem to react. As they soared up, he felt a joy he had never imagined a human could feel.

God must be laughing at me now, he thought, if there even was a God in this whole new existence he had found. Whatever the corpse in the forest meant, whatever was happening to the little world that had been everything to him until just a day ago, he was with the birds now – and they were leaving.

DOC B

BY LESLEY WARREN

It's five o'clock on Tuesday and I'm with my shrink.
I didn't wash my hair last night because Number 7 Phantasiestraße always reeks of cigarette smoke. I regularly joke to myself that its sole inhabitant is several orders of magnitude madder than I am. He's that kind of snowy-haired, jowly level of old that could put him anywhere between his late fifties and his early seventies; he wears fancy silk cravats in winter and he's always sighing as though the whole weight of the world rests upon his shoulders, dropping things and shouting *'Scheiße!'* despite the fact that he's French.

True to form, this week he lets me in and flits around like a demented moth, scanning my health insurance card in the back room, grumbling, violently shuffling papers like they've personally offended him in some way.

His apartment, at least, ties in with my preconceived notions of a therapist's lair. The big names jostle for space on his floor-to-ceiling bookshelves – Kant, Jung, and, yes, Freud. A strategically placed box of tissues I've so far left untouched sits on the patient-side table, beside fresh flowers. This week they are white and delicate and scentless.

'Mmm!' Doc B says with a polite society smile, returning and settling at last. 'So how have you been?'

I wriggle closer to the edge of the seat. Its last occupant was evidently a cat owner, and I don't want to fluff up my blouse. 'Um, good, actually.'

I wait. He waits. He visibly checks the clock.

Wryly I admit, 'I'm not sure what I should say.' This is so awkward. I always feel self-indulgent and weak here; a millennial snowflake who can't deal with her own brain. The very concept of therapy seems embarrassingly bourgeois.

His response doesn't exactly help. 'Well, if you're doing well, what is there to talk about?'

'I did feel pretty detached yesterday at the theatre,' I offer. 'I knew it was something I should have enjoyed, but somehow I wasn't... *present* enough to find it funny. That's the one thing still troubling me. The depersonalisation.'

He makes a little *so what* moue. 'It's natural you'll feel like that if you're very isolated all the time. You live alone, no boyfriend any more...'

'Yes,' I interject to get him off this all too familiar track – he often seems more in love with my ex than I ever was – 'but I felt like this when I lived with my parents, too. There but not there.' My mouth crimps at the edges. 'It's been eleven years now, actually.'

'Well, that makes sense,' Doc nods sagely. 'You've always kept to yourself; you've never had friendships, you've never connected with people – hence your failed relationship.'

I'm rather offended at this summary retelling of my past. 'That's not in any way true.'

'Oh!' He seems genuinely surprised. 'Then I think what *you* mean by depersonalisation is entirely different from what *I* mean. *You* only mean unreality. *Unwirklichkeit.*'

For months now – it *is* months, even though this is only the third time we've met – we've been struggling to get on the same page. For a moment I am positive this is the breakthrough we've been working towards. Emboldened, I ask, 'So how would *you* describe depersonalisation?'

He spreads his hands as though it's obvious. 'An inability to do anything. You wouldn't be able to have relationships or hold down a job if you were depersonalised.'

But... Frustration grits my teeth. *'Doch...!'*

As we acknowledge our stalemate, I realise this is the most openly I've ever seen him smile. We grin ruefully at each other like a couple of singles who've reached their third date and realised that beyond a penchant for psycho-philosophical debate, they have absolutely nothing in common.

'Maybe you should see someone else,' the shrink says, not unkindly. He sits back and folds his arms, plump and grandfatherly in the low suburban light.

White noise fills my head. I'm floundering, adrift on a cold tide. *What?*

His sympathetic smile widens as he draws in the empty life ring. 'There are problems even I can't solve.' He scribbles down a couple of names for me. 'Email me; let me know what they say,' he says a little wistfully, a stumped detective forced to abandon a case. Then a sudden last thought lights up his eyes. 'Do you have orgasms?'

Dumbfounded, I flush. *Congrats, Doc B. You've just scored a full house in my mental Cliché Bingo.*

'Then you're not depersonalised!' he repeats, but he's shaking his head indulgently as he grasps my hand. 'Ah, *Frau Warren.* You're the biggest puzzle I've had in years,' he chuckles, seeing me to the door.

Released with half an hour of my session to spare, I'm fairly dazed. I don't know what to think, how to feel. *Orgasms, indeed. What a farce.* Blinking, I wind my way out of the residential labyrinth – the wrong way at first – then walk briskly down the main road, enter the supermarket, where normal functional people stroll around with their normal functional brains. *Must be nice.* I don't look them in the eye; I wonder what they see in mine.

The hot summer light glints off car windscreens as I walk home, swinging my milk and bread. I could (should?) be crushed, but I realise I'm unnervingly fine; actually, I'm tickled pink. It could be something out of a sitcom. I can hear the laugh track now. *Dumped by my own therapist. That's pretty special.* I could skip down the pavement, perform a balletic leap, the tension of those sessions dissipating like dust in the wind, because I'm free. *No more trying to contort myself to fit a stranger's worldview.*

It doesn't help my problem in the slightest, but that's nothing new. If you never get your hopes up you'll never be disappointed – and deep down, beneath the thin veneer of hope, the realist in me was always expecting nothing.

Ah well. Give it another six months and maybe I'll be baffling Doc C.

DREAM OF A LAKE HOUSE
BY MARTIN GAMBLE

It took four days to arrive at the lake house. My only guide was a coordinate, a set of numbers that had been sent to my Codix, an internal memory transponder that connected me with other trainee Guardians in my Platoon. My Platoon that I had now abandoned, breaking my life's ambition as if it were a mirror. We had been on a training exercise in the middle of a forest, up to our eyeballs in shit, icy lakes, trekking up heavy torrents that almost made our calf muscles burst. At one point my arms, which were exposed by my vest top, had turned purple with the cold; thank God for the pain-deflector pill that we get before training. I had been heading towards target Z49, one target away from a completed training exercise mission, when something clicked inside my head that made me go cross-eyed; something had changed, a new idea I thought at first or an unearthed line of code that had surfaced to ensure my training success. The green light behind my eyeball had changed to red. It flooded my veins. Danger was my initial thought, of course, but I thought differently when I felt my heart turn black. But this was a training exercise, and there was and never had been a

Code Red. I deemed it unlikely that the Commander had changed something to throw off our danger senses – he's just not that much of an intuitive programmer – so I ran. I ran for the safety of both me and my Platoon. I ran through the woods. My long legs propelled me like a galloping horse that had been scared by a sudden noise, the muscles in my legs bulging, aching, but not relinquishing. I dodged the trees like I was in a pinball machine, sometimes smashing into tree trunks, causing scratches and bruises, even a nosebleed, but I never stopped. Running and running, blindly, until I realised I was no longer running from danger, but running away from the Platoon, breaking the oath that I could never retake. For the first time in my life, I was on my own, and sweat, maybe even a tear, trickled down my gaunt face at the thought that I could never go back. All I could see as the rising command in my Codix were the numbers of the digital coordinates, the ugly red glow of my warning light, lighting the backdrop as if the blood of a thousand men had stained every tree, every leaf and every organism in the forest.

During the four days of travelling, I rested occasionally and briefly, stopping to sleep for one hour each dawn. On the fourth morning, I was slowing as the night broke with a glimmer of daybreak that emphasised the details of the forest – the mist in the trees, an owl that turned its wide-eyed head to watch me as I ran past, my bloody stained uniform, torn from brambles, protruding sticks and sharp rocks. As I scoured the area, looking for a decent place for my morning rest, the trees gave way to open space, the immense expanse of the lake greeted me for the first time like a gaping open mouth that I could look deep down into and see a heart beating within the earth below. The lake reflected the silver sky and a single fish popped up out of the water and plopped back down as fast as it had appeared. I stepped on a twig and the snap echoed through the valley, disturbing a charm of magpies that flew off to find a new stretch of trees.

To my left, on the inner side of a simply-made wooden jetty, stood the lake house. It looked functional and unpretentious. The colour of the logs used for its construction matched the backdrop of line after line of trees, with a splattering of leafy plants and moss smeared onto the walls for extra camouflage. I walked towards it, agog as the coordinate countdown reached zero as I approached the house. I grabbed backwards over my shoulder for my rifle, squeezing the trigger that made the veins in my arms flow, my skin saturated from lack of nourishment. Upon opening the front door, my thoughts focused on a spot to rest, to stay still and bask in the zero coordinates that I had finally discovered as if they formed a warm blanket around me. Inside, the lake house was small, a single seat in the far corner, a sink and stove placed underneath the single window, plus a feeble looking table that someone had crafted from thick stumps and a row of thin branches woven together to make the top. The metre-wide bedroom had a single bed and another modest window that overlooked the lake and mountains. The early winter blew harshly, a wind that must have gathered momentum through the valley to finally batter against the front face of this rather sparse-looking shack.

On the far edge of the table, originally out of view, tightly wrapped around two opposing hooks, I saw a Blue-Blue Dream Cable, the type they had forbidden us to use in our training. They had warned us that if any of us were ever caught even in possession of such a forbidden item, then we would be sent to Exclusion without trial. Nobody had ever mentioned the words Blue-Blue Dream Cable again, yet now, before my very eyes, was the item that could bring forward my termination.

I couldn't resist. My hardened face muscles began to soften

as if I were comforting a child as I looked in awe. I unwound the cable from the hooks and, for the first time since the winter training had started, I felt a lightning bolt of ice shoot in different directions throughout my body, telling me that the effects of the pain-deflector pill were drawing to a close. I dropped the cable back onto the table. I took a step back as if my morals had become a boxer and had taken a swipe at me. The squawk from a small group of geese fighting outside squeezed through the gaps in the walls, and I looked out of the window to where they were swimming. For a moment, I envied the lives of the birds on and by the water. How simple an existence to live a life without temptation. A life of purity, mutual respect and the prerequisite of an animal hierarchy. But my stare towards nature was marred with the image of the Blue-Blue Dream Cable that had now been graffitied into my mind. The cable was everything I had ever wanted, but also the start of every possible nightmare that a being like me could possibly fathom. I already knew that the connector was compatible with the access port in the back of my head. There was no doubt that this cable had been put there for me and for me alone. Its power was immense. I wanted it, and it wanted me. I had never been in love before, but the cable was coaxing my heart to beat faster, to melt into liquid as it seductively whispered my name into my ear.

I took one last look out onto the lake, then took the two paces needed for me to grasp the cable again. My breathing deepened, a heavy pulsating feeling dominated my pelvis, the floodgate of blocked emotions and defective programs starting to release as tears began to stream down my face, and I wept. Me, a Guardian, now disconnected from his Platoon, planted by a lake house without a purpose. I took the Blue-Blue Dream Cable, reached around the back of my head with both arms, and plugged the device into my access port.

Light. Warmth. Sunshine. Peace.

'We have eagerly awaited your arrival. You are the first to arrive.' The voice sounded soothing and familiar, as if it were the voice of my mother.

But I couldn't remember ever having a mother.

I was still in the lake house, looking out of the window to the picturesque view of the water and mountains, but now the sun was streaming down into the valley, bouncing off the lake as it left a platter of shimmering diamonds on the water's surface, the warmth comforting my skin as it shone through the open window. The musical birdsong from outside bounced against the playful sound of splashing water as a heron fished for its breakfast on the water's edge. The lake was now teeming with life, an array of birds swam on the water, geese, ducks, doves, ospreys; a badger scurried on the ground outside and I could see deer grazing on the other side of the lake. Inside the cabin was a modern kitchen, eggs sizzling in a frying pan, fresh coffee dripping from the percolator; golden brown toast popped up from the toaster. Behind me was a large polished oak dining table that could seat eight people, eight chairs, eight empty spaces.

I walked towards the table and ran my fingers along the top, feeling the immense smoothness of such a fine varnished table. I looked round to see the door of the lake house opening, a dark figure of a man standing there as the bright summer's sun shone behind him in contrast. He walked towards me, his facial features revealing himself as he escaped the sunshine that poked through the trees, and, although I did not recognise him, he smiled as he opened his palm to reveal another Blue-Blue-Dream-Cable.

'Welcome, Guardian, you are the second to arrive,' said the motherly voice. We both sat down at the table, locked eyes on each other, and without words, told each other the story of our own lives. As the breakfast cooked and the smell of coffee permeated with the smell of warm foliage from outside, we sat in silence, waiting for the other Guardians to arrive.

GEMS OF A KIND

BY IAN STOUT

A shallow pool of water reflected the glare of Alex's flashlight. Underneath the water's surface there lay a bed of gems that shone with all the colours of the rainbow, and one shade that the human eye had never seen before.

Alex laughed boyishly and stomped over the gems. To his left, further down the yawning maw of the cavern, was a column of earth. It glistened with centuries of calcium. There was a sword plunged into the stone. Along the length of steel was a flowing script in a dialect centuries old, proclaiming that whoever bore the sword could never be slain in battle.

Alex slapped the sword's pommel and continued down the cavern.

A stone table waited for him. Atop it lay a ruby-red apple. There were two bite marks. Eve and Adam were cast from paradise just to taste this apple. It was there just for Alex, beckoning him forward with the red glare of eternal life.

Alex was not hungry, so he slapped the apple off his table. The fruit withered the moment it touched ground.

Across from Alex sat a woman. She did not shine like the most precious stones, promise conquest like artisan steel, nor could she offer him eternal life. But she was his, and he was hers – and to Alex – that love was more precious and fragile than any treasure.

She glared at him, but her eyes were smiling.

'You're rubbish at hide-and-go-seek, you know that?'

HEATDAYZE

BY JENNY BURNS

She leant out of her window into the dark. She loved watching those passing below from her perch four storeys above. Drawn to the glow emanating from the houses around her, and with the protection of the street between them, she peered into the living quarters of people she knew nothing of but must have passed a hundred times. Shared scenery, different lives – the windows to which were now quite literally thrown open. The heat that wrapped itself around her, around this city, like a thick, invisible cloud dissolved in it all guarding behaviours of domestic life. Even clothes, in some cases. Windows and curtains open, lights on, she watched as they moved around their flats. Observing their late-night habits, she could see them cook with their lovers, drink with their friends, watch the reflection of their TVs flicker across the walls.

There was not the slightest breeze; the air outside stood completely still and was barely more pleasant than indoors. She clasped her glass of rum, rotating it gently to watch the slow amber liquid crawl up the sides of the glass. She was conscious of the fact that her favourite indulgence on nights like these did not have the best of reputations. Loneliness, so often seen wearing the mask of despair, was a discreet rebellion.

The sun's night time echo radiated off the tar, the bricks, the concrete like the warmth of another too close and not close enough. She wondered if she could hear cicadas or if her mind was tricking her, so strong the association between their oscillating rhythm and these temperatures. Unmistakable, the sound of the sirens, the police car, in semi-distance, speeding through the darkness. Her body was in disbelief that anyone could have energy for criminal activity in this weather. Her mind knew better. What she loved about the heat was the state of exception it induced. In public conventions, in daily routines, and in her mind. It produced an unbalanced haze, which, as much as she enjoyed it, she knew did nothing to lower the rate of violent crime. A fire had been laid to the wooden pavilion in the park just the other week. Arson was the most reasonable assumption. It had to be a different type of madness that craved its satisfaction only in flames. This heat bred heat.

And this heat freed our lives after sunset. Something about its warmth gave the illusion of safety, robbed us of our fear of the dark and flung the night wide open for everyone. Unable to sleep comfortably, it created a city that hibernated during office hours but came alive after the scorching sun fell apart across the horizon.

Inverting the normal human rhythm, it was after hours that the town burst alive, that all the human energy, restless from the stifled desire and over-ready for release, roamed the streets and filled the open spaces. The town squares overflowed with bodies laughing, talking, draped over benches, hunched over kerbstones. Joyful and angry. Laughter and voices drifted and bounced corner to corner.

She made her way to the kitchen and refilled her glass. After giving herself a minute to enjoy the cool tiles against her bare feet, she returned to her metropolitan Olympus. The heat gave you a whole world, brought everyone's presence unbearably close, made people's spaces and their careful demarcations shift into each other. There was no protection. Suddenly we were a different species, living towards this world. All spaces were everybody's. All bodies were everybodies. And like all moments of exception, it held a hyper-realness that could fill you completely. It was impossible to cower and stiffen in the heat. It was easy to open wide and embrace.

Soon the rain would come, the thunderstorm they had all been waiting for. In fast forward the air would cool, the skies lose their burning intensity, the winds rise up out of nowhere, a sleeping giant roaring to life with an almighty force, capable of leaving the sun-drenched images only hours old a distant memory. Leaves would fly upwards off the trees, before the brief torrential rains would beat them down to the ground. The relief would be both exhilarating and foreboding.

This first messenger could still fascinate, rival the intensity of the summer sun with its ferociousness. It was what came after that would fill her with a mournful panic. The burnt amber would start leaching out of the sky into the trees, lungs would fill with the freshness of cooler air. The children would still play happily, grateful to be out again during playtime – blissfully unaware of the dying sun, the relentless churn of seasons, still unperturbed by the brutal march of time. Everyone else would know. Winter would reach out, slowly forcing layers of protection, wrapping us up, hiding us from each other again.

But that was not yet. Today's rain had come and passed – she had searched it for a perceptible trace of the coming change and had found none. Instead, its dampness infused the heat with another level of heaviness. It had brought not the cold but delivered air that stuck to your skin and your lungs, making you gasp from its warmth. She wanted to breathe it in deeply, into her very centre, and hold it inside her. Maybe tomorrow it would end. Any day now.

IFE

BY ILONA AHONEN

Her name is Ife. Lips too thick to be beautiful, but yet so feminine, so pretty. Exactly the kind of girl child who is good at sports and can wear all shades of pink and lilac so that it *really* looks good and not just like the typical pile of girly junk you see on any brat.

She must be no older than nine or ten, but she is tall for her age, and poised and lean. I love her, and am so flattered when she wants *me* to help her with her homework, and not the other volunteers.

Ife tells me about her gymnastics practice, and how they put makeup on them before a show. I can imagine the sequins glittering around her eyes, representing the enchanting world that I, with my poor athletic ability, could only dream of. As an adult in a teacher role, I love to bond with these popular girls, because I was never able to be one.

What if she gets attached to me and then I'm just gone? I wonder if she has a safe and supportive home, because aren't kids disadvantaged in this part of town? Of course, her parents might be doctors or lawyers for all I know.

I finally get a job, for two months at least, and leave Red Cross behind. Like Ife's parents probably did, I am moving to another country for better prospects. I never see her again.

IRREVERENCE

BY KRYSTA BROWN

Manah hadn't meant to summon the red spirit from the stone.

A slight of nature had led her to discover the demon's well-kept secret. She had been crushing a root, pounding the gleaming white slab in one hand against the rough grey block she had found on the riverbed. One strike and a spark of light released the warm, bright spirit from its hidden abode. A few clumsy attempts, and the wisp alighted onto the dried grass and willow bark she kept with her. Before, she had only known this spirit to come from the sky, from where it would lash out its tongue to feverishly devour trees, bushes and entire meadows.

Its spirit is hungry from the difficult journey into our world, the young woman thought. Yet the more she fed him, the more voracious his appetite became. She ventured several times to gather more of its preferred nourishment. Twice she had erred. Once, in feeding it the tender green ferns, causing the spirit to immediately sputter in protest and threaten to return to wherever it had come. And again as she overstepped some invisible boundary, leaning in over the entrancing figure until he, too, had reached out to her, curling toward her long black hair and beckoning her toward him – only to punish her intrusion with a brief but terrible lash of his orange tongue.

This spirit has chosen me. An overwhelming sense of power came with this revelation, emanating from her new demon friend and seeping into her. Like a fever, she could feel its smouldering within her. In her village, only the circle of elders had the authority to control the hearth, which they guarded zealously and fed continuously to keep the spirit satisfied. In exchange, the demon allowed them to place the spoils of the hunt over its writhing arms, transforming raw and bleeding carcasses into mouthwateringly tender morsels. This ardent spirit was the lifeblood of her people, and their routine revolved around keeping its essence fed and satisfied. In turn, it offered its warmth, its usefulness and protection against the beasts of the night. Its presence was sacred.

Yet not one of the grizzled elders could summon him at will.

Instead, as Manah knew from the elders' stories, they relied on guidance from their totem, the firehawk, for the chance to harness him. A flash of white from the sky, touching down to light a parched tree, sent the entire tribe into a frenzy, not only because of the very real danger of the unpredictable sprite spreading to their encampment, but also to bring part of it back with them. *The firehawk taught us how to steal away the red spirit*, she thought, stroking the carved totem amulet around her neck. The majestic birds knew when it would appear, and used its power in the hunt, carefully grasping blazing limbs in their talons and spreading the grateful spirit to the bleached grassland, where it devoured the yellowed stalks and left a trail of unwary victims in its wake. *A feast for the firehawk, as well as for her people.* The hawks' revelation had so profoundly transformed their way of life, they lived in eternal gratitude to the rapturous predators.

And now she, who had herself not yet even produced a new

human life, could call forth the giver of life itself from two simple stones.

Should I tell the elders? Manah thought uneasily. As a woman, tribe law forbade her from managing the hearth, except to prepare meals over its gaping maw. Guarding the spirit itself was another matter. It was unnatural, they would say, even blasphemous. *No,* she decided.

The seasons passed, and Manah privately trained her skill, becoming so adept she could welcome her friend in a flash. The stones, and the secret they contained, became her constant companions. This she guarded within the pit of her heart as zealously as the elders harboured the remnants of the last wildfire.

Yet a time came when water from the sky extinguished the firehawk's gift, and her people were expelled from the spirit's favour and cast into darkness.

It is time, Manah decided. Huddled in the damp, she summoned her friend before a sceptical and increasingly captivated audience. In the growing light, many eyes meeting hers shone with elation, awe and gratitude. Yet some could not hide their suspicion, and their envy. One strike of the stones had upturned the familiar order. The elders who controlled the firehawk's gift and the male watchers could feel the instability of their role as sole guardians of the light. They had become irrelevant – and at the hands of a half-grown woman.

✳

As the professor dusted away the layers of earth from the last skeleton, he felt as if its charred remains whispered to him the last moments of a long forgotten folk. An entire tribe – men, women and children – had met the same fiery fate within the confines of the cave. *Amazing,* the archaeologist thought to himself. *Based on the blackened bones and these particular stones here,* the archaeologist deduced, *I'd say this young male had used quartz and pentlandite to start a fire – predating all previous evidence of this primitive method by at least 10,000 years!*

But the attempt must have gone awry, he could see. The fire consumed first a young woman, whose crumbling remains lay nearby, before making its way to the mouth of the cave, blocking the exit for many of the other tribe members. As he moved forward to examine the nearby figure, he could clearly see the greyed skull, its temporal bone partially exposed on the cave floor. Suddenly, a jagged and savage gash caught his attention. The skull had been brutally damaged. *Like looking at a prehistoric crime scene,* the professor thought, piecing the clues together. Sifting through the dust where the woman's bones lay, his fingers unearthed a stone carving – two wings, spread wide below a curved beak. *A revered spirit, perhaps?*

KNOCK ON ANY DOOR
BY NINO KHUNDADZE

The burning feeling all over his body became unbearable. He had to open his eyes to check what was going on. He tried, but he was unable to do it. Brightness made him stay in the dark for a while. Slowly, he got used to light and was able to observe the world around him. Nothing seemed familiar. The long beach seemed so empty, empty of people, empty of memories. It felt like meeting a stranger; somewhere deep inside you recognise him, but still, you don't. He found shelter under a huge old tree. Now he could think.

But who was he? Who was that person who almost got burned on the beach a few minutes ago? How did he get there? Where was he? He felt like a huge book full with empty pages. He could not remember the name of the book, what it was about, where did it belong? There was just emptiness.

He decided to walk. It felt like the only way out of the puzzle. After minutes or hours of walking, he came to a huge building that seemed very familiar. He did not know why, but he knew he could find answers there, even if he had to knock on any door.

LAUGHTER AT THE LORD OF SILENCE
BY SVEN HENRICHS

Once upon a time we thought each thing had a certain purpose, a hidden meaning. We thought the same about words and sentences. And we started to search for treasures in language. Determining good or bad reasons to argue this or that purpose or meaning captivated us. Grammar deluded us many times, and our findings had nothing else to offer than conventionalised lies. The hidden treasures presented themselves as a set of arrangements to the audience whose contractors had died out. We desperately hoped to decipher the logic behind our grammar. But that knowledge died with them. Studying the logic of grammar may be a pleasant time-killer for someone who is interested in tracking trails of lies back down through centuries. Presupposing you like to be compelled to trust a silent treaty unquestioned. And they all lived happily after. And not forever.

Today we know: meaning and purpose need the focus to be placed on shaping and reshaping, pairing and repairing. Otherwise you sit, trust the laws, and later disappear into where you came from.

Two planets meet each other in outer space.

'Oh man, we haven't seen each other for ages. How are you?'
'To tell the truth, not so well.'
'Really? What's up?'
'...I got homo sapiens.'
'Don't worry, had it too – what occurs by itself will go away by itself!'

See: reality always regains predominance. And it always edges illusion out. A matter of time, though. To ignore the nature of language is to close one's eyes to reality. You better know precisely when to afford it. You seldom get away unharmed with lifelong daydreaming. This clue was probably the decisive last push for me to leave the Army of the Lord. And I was initiated to another group of humans simultaneously without recognising it. I joined the group of those who like to decide by themselves in which kind of narration they want to believe, in which kind of story they want to live. Biophysical causalities, economic improvements, or political decisions, to us, have lost their meaning. We avoid the security of handing ourselves over to an implicit silence, we reject cushioned academic armchairs. We prefer the adventures of designing reality ourselves. And that can't be done in silence.

The Origins of the Word stay hidden behind a veil of silence. They work their way through the coverings to create fear. Fear shall make you run and flee. Fear shall take your breath away and keep you from speaking. The Lord of Silence and his comrades are well aware how to operate these weapons. We don't run. We face it. We grasp the word. And we fight every kind of menace by laughing at it. In return we receive a fireplace where we can warm our hands on frosty nights, where you might have a peaceful plate of *penne all'arrabbiata*, where you can relax from all that killing. And we've done that ever since we lived at the bottom of the cliff or in a cave. If we were lucky, we sat at the open fire with hopefully one bite of meat per month for each member of the clan. Apart from that, our sparse menu card mainly consisted of roots and berries gathered in the nearby forest, scraped knees from daily gathering included. At these times, there can't have been many reasons for a good laugh. Nevertheless, at some point we found out.

Beware of poisonous snakes! a sign may have said on the path back to your cave. And, bringing home the harvest of one full day's work, carefully carried in cupped hands, off they flew, the berries. They flew up, eyes wildly searching down in the meadow for a winding beast. The giggling of the signer caused short relief. And a little outburst of rage probably followed immediately.

Origins as untouchables enable any of us to use their power. Dear Lord of the Silence, the King of Nothing does that. His army is inhabiting our world, reigning our world ever since. Spreading fear and trying to force us into certain actions, making you repeat them so many times that you do not question their legitimacy anymore. Or did you ever question the right of your local church to tell you stories about generations that last approximately seven hundred years, as Abraham's does?

The power in this reign of silence works with screams, stabbings, punches, tortures, war and blood. It spills guts not only if it is necessary. The force of this silence is violence. It covers wounds with the next pain, sending out a relentless follow-up of needle stitches, whip bruises, nails through bones and so on. That's the bloody old-fashioned way. Nowadays, the troops of The Holy Lord are working on us in a more civilised matter. They perfected methods because times change. They were compelled to acknowledge life as a value in itself, and so a dead enemy became a bad enemy. Corpses can't work for anybody any more. What a pity. So they found ways to kill you by keeping you alive. Therefore, you have to work, be of use, be productive, perpetuate your social life. That's what they reward you with. Now try to laugh about that.

Two mayflies are sitting and one of them complains:

'What a shitty day. All morning I had to learn how to fly, than I had a rotten apple for lunch, and now the old-age home is waiting for me.'

The other one did not answer. It had dropped dead already.

Language and words survived the Stone Age, Greek antiquity, the Middle Ages and modern times. We survived too, The Army of Light, guerrillas of the spoken word. And reality did, of course, too. The threat of thirty-inch incisors protruding from wide open jawbones transformed into a cascade of war states. Today sabre-toothed tigers wear three thousand euro business suits, and they don't even look expensive. They tell the driver of the limousine where all the sitting ducks are to be found today. On the way they stop for a double espresso at a trendy Italian bar.

We have to speak up because death by silence is no choice. We laugh at the limo passenger, we laugh at stock interests, we laugh at loans, we laugh about heads of government with their thumbs on red buttons. We even laugh at our old-age home. Maybe they are bitter laughs, but we are still laughing. So when the nurse asks me about the state of my bed-pan on my deathbed, I would like to be able to answer, 'Mind your own shit!'

Although she surely would not deserve that sentence.

LET LOOSE

BY IAN STOUT

Val draws back her bowstring and releases. She never holds more than a second to shoot. Wait any longer and she might question her aim.

The arrow buries in a red sun. Sounds of oak ring across the stands, through the ears of the audience, and are lost in the corners of a tent. A roar spreads through the crowd. They stamp and holler, and throw flowers at her feet.

A boy, they marvel, *he won the Carnival.*

Val bows her head to accept a medal round her neck. Her face is stone.

The streets of Venice know her better than anyone else. Water splashes over the lip of cobblestones and mists her bare feet. The cold is her friend. It seeps into her bones and sees her spirit. Not a boy destined to shoot arrows until his back gives. No. Here she is a name and not a number.

Statues of dragons line the corridor. She walks between them as an equal. Their marble scales are cool to the touch. One dragon grins at her. She lays her bow at its feet. Underneath talons the oaken weapon cowers. Here her archery makes her no better than anyone else.

She steps up and straddles the dragon's back. Ice seeps into her skin.

Val opens her mouth. Her lips loose her true name like an arrow.

'Val,' she cries, smiling.

NOTHING

BY ANURAG

nothing
/nʌθɪŋ/

Word Origin
- Before 'words', 'time' and 'god'

Definitions
1. Exact opposite of 'everything'
Not god.
Not abstract.
More than what we know,
Exact opposite of 'everything'

Example:
He never quite believed
In the theory of Guardians. He was born without one.
A child was a child, meant to be in this world, for one reason or the other. Guardians are luxury, but children grow nevertheless. He travelled across the cosmos, barefoot, as a child, eating stars and leaving footprints on all the fifty-three moons of Jupiter.

He was limitless and yet in control. There was no pavement he wouldn't walk, no tree he wouldn't climb, no flower he wouldn't smell and no fruit he wouldn't eat. His heart would dangle by a hook for hours in the sea of unknown, waiting for a fish to come to take it. Many came, conquered, lost in the process, surrendered to his will and to his wisdom. He was everything and everything was him.

He went on to become a god. A god is definitely higher than a Guardian. A god doesn't need a Guardian.

But that changed when he fell in love and let life come to him as a newly born.

As he retired from godship into guardianship, fears followed. He began to believe in higher powers and turned into a priest.

He lived differently now. Bound, blind and scared.

He realised he knew nothing. He was nothing and nothing was him. *Everything* he once had made no sense. Courage became stupid as his bones began to tremble every now and then.

He didn't want his child to walk barefoot. Shoes were important, the cosmos too dangerous. Not all pavements were worth walking and flowers often were poisonous (and sometimes carnivorous).

With time, moss has grown around his feet. He eats now only the food he knows, drinks only fresh water from the lake nearby. He finds it funny how his child wants to fly with doves and dragons. No one should try that and there are no dragons.

Only if, for once, children listened to their guardians.

    2. Exact opposite of 'love'
        Not dislike
        Not at all hate,
        An apathetic acedia.

Example:
Maybe your hum
Could just fall off now.
It has been hanging there, big-eyed monster,
Patronising me, holding on my lower lip
Like a newly born orangutan.
Trying to find life where it doesn't exist.
I have been a corpse all my life,
My lips are dry and purple,
There is nothing to kiss.
Absolutely nothing.

> 3. Exact opposite of 'expectation'
> Not despair
> Not desperation,
> A despondent disappointment,
> Exact opposite of 'expectation'

Example:
She looked out.
And there was nothing. She had wished for a window seat all her life and here she was, with all the view to herself. But nothing was left to be seen, nothing at all. Not in a metaphorical way. Everything was gone, lost, or never existed. She couldn't tell.
Her train ran and ran faster than ever. She wanted to catch a breath, capture a few photographs of her present, before it turned into her past.
But the speed was such that her camera was lost in her eyes, her tears too which came out of pain, just stayed on her lids and flowed back in.
Everything was disappointing about this sight. This superlative sight she had always wished for. All she was left with was an

empty train, a window seat and a lifetime to stare at nothing. Absolutely nothing.

    4. Exact synonym of 'man'
        Too proud,
        Strutting towards his end
        Almost invisible in front of life
        Exact synonym of man

<u>Example:</u>
On the board of chess,
We march,
Mere pawns,
Other pieces stand behind,
A battle is about to begin,
An earthquake strikes,
Everyone flies, dies, ends up in a box.
Maybe tomorrow we get another chance,
If life wants to play.

PARKING SUNS

BY ERIKA SURAT ANDERSEN

Tanya holds her mother's hand as they walk down the hallway towards her ailing grandfather's bedroom. She didn't want to come, but Mama promised they'd go to the Smokehouse afterwards, the best burger place in the world, so she agreed. She's really hungry and hopes they won't stay long.

She doesn't exactly understand what's wrong with her grandfather – *Opa*, as she calls him – but her parents talked late last night in the kitchen when they thought she was asleep and couldn't hear. They kept talking about *Parking Stones* or *Parking Suns*, or something like that. What did that mean? A *Parking Stone*? Maybe Opa ran over a big stone in a parking lot and hit his head on the roof of his car. But he didn't even drive, so that didn't really make sense. Or a *Parking Sun*? A sun that was parked and never moved? But the sun does move, at least at the end of the day, when it sets, so she's not sure.

When they enter the room, her mother stops right away. There's Opa, lying in bed. The bones in his face and hands really stick out now – even more than last time – and his eyes aren't blue anymore. They're grey.

'Oh, Daddy, you need to eat more.' Mama's voice is shaky. Tanya hopes she won't start crying again.

'Hi, Kiddo,' Opa says, in a creaky voice. Tanya thinks it's funny to hear her mom being called a kid.

Mama bends down to hug Opa and kisses him on the cheek. Papi puts his hand on Opa's shoulder. The plastic bag with pee is still at the foot of the bed – Tanya finds that disgusting and wishes Mama or Papi would cover it up.

Opa looks at Tanya and her older sister, Elise. 'Hiya, kids,' he says, in that creaky voice again. Then he starts to cough. It goes on a long time and they all have to wait for it to stop. Mama brings over his glass of water.

'How're you feeling – in between coughing fits?' Mama asks him.

Opa says, 'Could be worse.'

Mama gives a short little laugh. She pulls up a chair next to the bed and starts telling him about what the family's been doing since their last visit to America. Every once in a while Papi says something. Tanya looks over at her older sister, who – just like she knew she would – is slowly sneaking out the door and heading towards the living room, where the caretaker hangs out. He's usually on his cell phone or watching television, and Elise will probably join him.

Tanya goes over to Opa's desk, hoping to find the big pad of paper he keeps for her, ever since he found out she likes to draw. She remembers when his desk was full of books, papers and pens, but now it's covered with cotton pads, pill bottles, and that little machine that the doctor wraps tight around your arm. She's about to give up her search when she spots the pad of paper squashed between the wall and the desk. She pulls it out and finds her box of coloured pencils behind it. All still there.

She settles on the floor with the pad, smoothes out the wrinkles on the top page, and opens the box of pencils.

Today, she'll use every colour in the pack.

Tanya draws a brown-haired girl on a blue horse riding up a steep beige mountain covered with dark green trees. On top of the hill she paints a huge plate of orange sweet potato fries and a big bowl of red ketchup next to it, waiting for someone to dip the fries into it. Someone like her. She loves sweet potato fries. She then draws a purple dragon with grey ears, an aqua green ocean to the right of the mountain, and a sunset that stretches all the way from the left to the right, in red-orange, yellow, and pink. She's just about to add magenta when she realises everyone's stopped talking.

Tanya looks over at the bed. Her mother is quiet, just holding Opa's hand, and her Papi is looking at the floor. Her grandfather stares straight ahead. Tanya's pretty much finished with her drawing, so she holds up the big pad at the foot of Opa's bed, where his eyes seem to be looking.

She decides to tell him the story of her picture.

'In this magical but sad kingdom, they've completely run out of sweet potato fries. There's only one plate of orange fries left in the whole world and it's on top of a mountain, guarded by a big and scary dragon. And ever since the sweet potatoes ran out, the sun hasn't set.'

Tanya can't tell if Opa is listening, but Mama and Papa are, so she keeps going. 'Everyone is afraid of the dragon except for this cowgirl, who's very brave. She rides up the hill with her sword and fights the dragon and wins! After that she eats a couple of the fries – just to make sure they're okay – then sticks some of them into the ground. Suddenly sweet potato plants start to grow all over the fields. The cowgirl jumps on her horse, carrying the plate that still has a lot of fries on it, and starts to go back. When she rides down the mountain, the sun starts to move – it's not parked anymore – and a really big sunset fills the sky and everyone's happy again.'

Tanya finishes her story. Her grandfather doesn't say anything and she doesn't think he heard her. But then he smiles. Really slowly and really big.

PERMIT

BY IAN STOUT

Our pilot informed us we were nearly in Chicago. Children clutched at armrests and cried like it was going out of fashion. A few passengers played a drinking game where they sipped wine every time a child cried. They were stone cold drunk in an hour. I envied them. Three months clean and my hands still shook at the sight of a red.

I risked a peek outside the window. Shades of sapphire blasted me. We were flying through a rainbow. I'd never thought it possible to come close to one – rainbows always fled from me, like sobriety.

My vision swam. There was colour, then sound, and then feeling.

A bee landed on my hand. It crawled as if searching for flowers.

'Go sting the child in 4C,' I told the bee.

'I'm not touching that brat,' said the bee. Its voice soothed me, strangely.

'You want some sugar?' I waved the stewardess down.

'Don't,' said the bee, 'airline sugar causes cancer.'

The stewardess came to my row. She asked me if there was anything I needed. I told her I needed to go home. She told me home was where the heart was. The cravings were my home – every night they screamed at me, like children. I was destined to spend a third of my life here.

She put a hand on my shoulder, and asked me – again – if I needed anything.

I ordered a glass of red. Sometimes there's nothing you can do.

SALVATION

BY MARION HERMANNSEN

The ocean spread like a liquid black mirror below the ship. The surface reflected a full moon, so clear in its pallid beauty that I could make out individual craters. I took a deep breath. *The calm before the storm,* the captain had called it, after listening to the OPC forecast. Storm force winds, he'd explained, before sending the crew to secure the boat.

They were asleep now, except for the old man in his cabin above the deck. I turned and waved, not sure if he could see me leaning against the railing. His grizzled appearance and decades of working the sea had earned him the respect of every one of his men. Outlined against the faint glow of his instruments, our captain steered us out of trouble, steady and unmoving as a figurehead.

My father had fished in the old country, long before industrial ships had moved in and killed off the local industry. He'd been one of the last to surrender. Rather than swap his life on the ocean with the oppressive stench of the cannery, he'd sold everything they'd owned and moved to the city.

Mom used to tell us about him: his dreams, his want for a better life for his kids. I remembered his eyes – blue-green like sea foam when he was happy, black-blue like the deepest ocean when he was angry. And I saw the yearning, the aching despair, when he watched nature programmes with us. I wasn't surprised when he went fishing one weekend and never returned. He might have turned his back on the sea, but the sea never let him go.

The stars above me shone like pinpricks in black velvet. There was no place as mystical as right here, floating above thousands of feet of seawater, mysterious and terrifying at the same time. The silvery globe below me rippled, then broke apart in a thousand glittering sparkles.

A drop hit my forearm. Then another. The trance I'd found myself in was broken. It was time. The storm was here. Sweet-tasting water found my face, my mouth, and I couldn't help licking the liquid from my lips. Icy-cold, refreshing, the droplets fell faster as I raced across the deck to sound the alarm.

Bleary-eyed men, zipping up their foul weather gear, fell into their routine. Within minutes, the gentle spray of rain had turned into a wall of black water, competing with its salty companion, rising from below. For a moment I closed my eyes, fighting an irrational feeling of displacement, of floating, until I felt the deck below my feet. I glanced up at the captain, relieved to see him at his usual spot at the helm. As long as he was calm, we were safe.

The trawler pitched violently. The waves weren't coming at us in a straight line, but danced around us, whipped by the storm. The wind bellowed down the deck and slapped me across both cheeks before moving on to find the next victim. At the next lurch, the ocean spat an ice-cold wave into my face. I shook myself like a dog and blinked. The captain held the boat on course, despite the sea's best effort to shatter us for its amusement.

I'd never experienced cold like this before. Despite the outrageously expensive bad-weather gear, rivulets of molten ice worked their way down my neck, under the collar, and ran icy spider fingers down my spine. My body valiantly tried to warm the constant trickle but was losing the battle.

Intermittent shivers prickled across my skin so quickly, my body was vibrating with tension. The roar of the water and the storm had deafened the crew hours ago. The first mate was shouting at me from only a few feet away. His mouth moved and his nostrils flared, but his words were swallowed by the continuous howl. It probably didn't matter anyway.

One by one, my senses were being overwhelmed by the onslaught. First my hearing, then my eyesight. The blanket of water pouring over me in regular intervals stole my vision as effectively as a blindfold. The only thing that reminded me I was still alive and not another washed-up piece of debris was the smell. Rancid dankness slapped my face every time a wave broke over me, mixed with ozone when I took a desperate breath.

The roar died down, a theatrical gesture as if nature itself wanted to prepare the stage for the most dramatic impact. I looked again at the captain. As I watched, he stood up. All movement around me stopped. I'd laughed when my father had called the sea an 'angry mistress.' What a silly notion, anthropomorphising water. Force of nature, yes, especially when the weather turned. But there was no emotion, no humanity in the wall building up in front of the trawler.

Every hand on deck was staring forward, upward. The towering water was beautiful. It was so high, it blocked the storm, and an eerie calm descended onto the boat. Close up, I admired the glassy smoothness of the wave, the black inkiness mixed with bottle-greens. I wished I could reach out and touch the ocean, my father's, *my* mistress. Higher and higher she climbed, until there was no more sky, nothing around us. Only the boat, its men, and our destiny.

She wasn't angry, this ruler over life and death. She would have her sacrifice, and there was nothing we could do about it. There was freedom in having the decision taken out of my hands. I smiled as she descended, faster and faster, offering me her kiss, my salvation.

SEASON SEQUINS

BY JUSTINA DEŠRIŪTÉ

Loveliest season of the year: the Christmas season. A time for endless consumption, jaws breaking with fake smiles, passive-aggressive drunk chats and a steady stream of lies. It's all about the happiness of seeing him or her. 'What talented children you have!', such an improvement in their screaming, *oh pardon*, singing, since last year. How deeply appreciated you feel getting yet another bottle of Bordeaux; which... you'll just pass on to somebody else later. To share the joy of the season, of course. Ah, yeah, all the publicly allowed lies. Such a pleasure to snack upon the jolly deceptions.

Santa? Of course we are not forgetting him! With the cookie-full belly sliding through the tall and graceful chimneys of lies! Just to dump some doomed-for-short-term-glory pieces of plastic, labelled as *toys*. Every single time I hear it, this word reminds me of Toi Toi cabins. Toys. Just something to be removed from your inner system after the value is taken out of it. Walking through the door of Tacenda, a decades-old pub with a decades-old crowd of mostly *hes* and an occasional *she*, I realise how much I could use a Toi Toi or, for that matter, just a regular loo. Frigging Christmas season with all the office cakes, cookies and eggnogs mixed with my lack of willpower to resist. I quickly wave 'hi' to Tom, the bartender, asking for 'the usual', and head directly towards the wooden door with a blurred-out painted sign of a skirt and pants next to each other. After ten minutes of getting all the sweet joys out of the system, I start to slowly wash my hands with brownish tap water. Once, twice, four times pressing an obviously empty soap dispenser, I knock it down in a short burst of rage. Less than five seconds later, I start crying. A few moments rush away and I try a deep breath in and immediately regret the decision. I start blinking intensely to clear my vision and desperately look around for a distraction to focus on. To forget. A used slimy bandage is lying on the side of the sink, glittering sequins spread here and there on the slippery floor tiles. I've always appreciated the honesty of bathrooms and the endless stories they tell. The place for inner exposure, for all types of outbursts. You can try to get it all out, to cover up the dirt, to leave it behind but you know it's still there. You still smell it.

Once back in the bar area, I notice that Tom has volumed up the music even though the pub is half empty. That means he doesn't want to talk. I also spot a camera lying next to my whiskey glass. Which explains things. I take a generous gulp of a drink and pick up a used Nikon. The battery indicator starts blinking red as I turn it on. Still enough power to step through several shots. Very well: it could be that it's the camera which will last longer out of the two of us. An unknown street full of red lanterns and grinning Asian kids. Me dipping my toes in freezing river water through the edge of a bamboo boat. Amy with a half-eaten strawberry between her chipped front teeth. Looking at me from the other side of the lens. Smiling. Still happy back then.

'Tom, was your daughter here just now?'

'No. Dropped it yesterday evening. Apologies for the cracked lens. Thinks it fell on the taxi floor during moving.'

'Was she alone?'

Tom pauses painfully.

'No.'

Just like in the bathroom, another wave of rage starts rising up. I asked for it. I will have to deal with it.

'Do you think she is happy now?'

'It's Christmas season, boy. Everybody pretends to look happy.'

Tom knows how to comfort me and still stay honest. I finish up the remaining whiskey in one sip.

'Do you think I will ever be happy enough to smile as genuinely, Tom?' I ask, staring at her photo as the red blinking intensifies.

Tom sighs impatiently and pretends that the ideally-polished bar tap needs extra brushes.

'Is this one of those times when you want me to lie to protect your delicate emotions?'

I smile as the wave calms down.

'I'll take another one, sir. To the season!'

SECRET

BY LIDIA GALLI

Kevin headed to the sofa. Katy took out her hiking shoes. Why had he decided to leave the city so suddenly for a place like this? Silent woods surrounded the cabin; a cold lake in front of it reflected the few birds brave enough to fly over that place. She turned around and took two steps toward the sofa, feeling the creaky floorboards bending under her weight. Kevin was staring at the ceiling. She was so tired of trying to read his mind! She needed air. She stepped outside wearing only her socks. He didn't ask her where she was going.

'After all, where could I go?' she sighed aloud, closing the door behind her. He hadn't rented a car from the train station, no, he had booked a cab. A cab! She thought it would have been a short ride. Three hours! Anyway, they didn't have a car, they were stuck. She walked down the porch stairs, sat on a huge rock next to the lake, and shivered.

'Brumous.' The word escaped from her mouth in a whisper. A grey sky filled with unfriendly heavy clouds was hovering over her. It was spring in the rest of the world, but here winter was still lingering around, like a guest that had overstayed his welcome. *Brumous*: a word her father loved. He was surely worried, they were supposed to meet today. She managed to send him a message asking for a rain check before Kevin took her mobile phone, purse and luggage to help her. As soon as they were settled, she wanted to call Dad to explain, but she was rushed into a two-hour hike in the woods.

She thought of that morning. He had burst into their flat with an unconvincing smile on his face, bubbling about a surprise trip for their fifth anniversary. Except that their anniversary had been six months before. Then, he just started packing for both of them, his movements too frantic to be mistaken for joy. His panicking made her panic too; she started throwing stuff in a suitcase, asking if she needed her passport and if she should pack summer or winter clothes. After two trains and the never-ending trip in the cab, they ended up in this place, wherever it was. What the hell was going on? Could it be he knew...?

The place was okay, though. She loved isolated places. When she was a child, she would spend a few days in the woods with her father almost every month. They didn't stop their trips even after that awful accident. One of her first memories: finding a dead man at night near their tent when she was seven. After that one bad experience, she had many wonderful ones that helped her almost forget about those empty and glossy eyes. She shivered. The woods that surrounded her seemed those from her memories, and her nightmares.

'I should have suggested a location.' She had begged Kevin for years for a trip outdoors, and now she had what she wanted in the worst possible moment: she was pregnant, or at least the pregnancy test from last night said so. She hadn't decided how to tell him yet. After all, he didn't want kids, and she didn't too, right? But there was someone inside her now, living because she was alive, protected and nurtured by her body. Life was easier that morning. Now she was pregnant, in the middle of nowhere, surrounded by her worst memories.

'Katy, do you want a cup of tea?' Kevin's voice seemed soft, relaxed. Maybe it was all her paranoia. She stepped inside. The cabin wasn't that bad. Most of the floors were covered with thick, soft carpets like the one warming her feet now, while the many watercolours on the walls painted by a certain D. O'Connery depicted the woods and lake in different seasons. She caressed an autumn painting near the entrance and wondered if they would come back to see the real thing one day. She looked over the table, a smile starting to blossom on her lips: her favourite tea, scones, fruit... Then she stared at Kevin on the sofa.

'Sit down, please.'

His eyes reflected the sky outside: cloudy, grey, troubled.

'What's going on, Kev?'

He unconsciously touched the black suitcase next to him, the one he guarded as a dragon would its lair. It contained his work files and whatever he needed to survive a day at the office, as he had explained to her a million times, but always refusing to open it.

'Listen, I...'

She sat down. She knew she would need to sit down for what was coming.

'You want to dump me?'

'What? No...'

He took the briefcase and opened it. She looked at it half amazed, half dying of curiosity. Inside there was a box, as black and as big as the briefcase itself. It had a tiny red button on it.

'So what happens if I press the button?' she asked, trying to sound playful, but feeling every cell in her body screaming to run away from that room.

'Nothing,' he replied. 'It's when you let go that things get nasty.'

He wasn't serious, was he? She looked in disbelief while her finger moved nearer and nearer the button, as a magnetic force was guiding it. She pressed it and the box sprang open. Kevin was breathing heavily.

'Just have a look.' And a look she had.

Police reports, newspaper articles and photos of murders. She thought of their baby. Would it know what Mommy was looking at? Feeling the horror she was feeling? Among those papers a familiar face: a photo of her father. She picked it up and noticed the one underneath it: it was that guy, the dead guy she found in the woods so many years ago. She stared at Kevin, all the unanswered questions struggling to become words.

'Katy, your father is a serial killer. His next victim could be you.'

SHABBIR

BY ANURAG

Nights are long this time of the year and I have just begun to light the fire. These December evenings are hard to pass if you don't torch some wood. As the red-blue flame blasts through the skin of dampened mango twigs, sequins fly. I have pushed my body dangerously close to it, sanguine for it to find in its heart, ways to melt this agonising pain in my bones. But the closer I am to fire, the more it patronises me. Shabbir was no different, now that I wonder. Patronising, petrifying and relentless with his green Kashmiri eyes.

Those eyes, and the long curly hair, almost like a woman's; they are to be blamed as far as my indulgence in this matter is concerned. Shabbir is the *Tacenda* of my life. It's the last new word I learned, only yesterday. An ancient word that has given a new meaning to my memories. *Things one must not talk about.* But I have been silent about Shabbir for far too long. Seventy-one years.

Seventy-one years ago, he was supposed to go Harsabad, but instead he had knocked on my door in Harsapur. That changed everything for him and me.

'Shabbir Hasrati.' He had sheepishly told me his name when we first met at the altar of my giant yellow mansion. His surname literally translated to *dreamer*. In those days, India was bustling with these dreamers. Everyone was dreaming. New nation, free nation. Nonsense stuff. As if something was going to change.

But in that way, Shabbir was the true prodigal son of his hallucinating motherland. Given his age and those times, I forgave him for his high talks that I knew were going nowhere, much like this country. If new political boundaries were to translate into the freedom of people, then freedom would have been ours a long time ago.

You see, this is the trouble with me. One, I am educated and, two, I am a first-class pessimist. I always must put forward my opinions and my opinions seldom sound warm. It also keeps my share of ego fed. After all, how many Bengali women born in 1916 could boast a graduate degree?

Shabbir was totally opposite in that sense. His education ended at some *Madarsa*, no further than the Quran and basic counting. He didn't have that kind of upbringing either which often makes people act in a certain way; to eat rice with spoons, to think twice before shaking hands. He was too naïve to be smart, too innocent to understand. No wonder he had landed in Harsapur.

Imagine his scenario. Someone had told this little orphan that Harsabad (and not Harsapur) was going to be a part of Pakistan once the freedom was granted. He sold his father's property, his mother's jewellery and his two goats, one male and one female (perfect to multiply the number) to arrange for a total of one thousand rupees and set off on his journey to Harsabad.

But when he reached the bus stand of his hometown of

Betiya, the dimwit sat in the bus to Harsapur. He only realised his mistake when he had thrown his luggage at Harsapur terminus, letting out a sigh as a huge amount of dust settled on his face. Our roads were always like that.

The address he was expecting to go to, of some Sukun Miyaan, didn't belong to this town. After roaming around the town for two days and spending most of his money, Shabbir knocked at my door.

He was a poet, he would tell me, though I never saw him writing a poem. He could hardly write to save his life. I was a fond reader of poetry. My library consisted of Shakespeare and Wordsworth and Shelley. They were my husband's collections but, after him, they were the only things I could truly call mine. He would write in Urdu.

I had never learnt Urdu. Urdu was a man's language. Transcribed in Persian, it was always considered too difficult for women to write. That's why, in the school's curriculum, even in the co-ed convents, women would be taught Bangla separately. For us, Urdu was just charming. Boys would throw Urdu poetry and one-liners at us and we would blush and giggle.

But Shabbir was not a good poet. His poems were always confused and about nation and full of anguish. Urdu is for romantics. A language of love. The way Shabbir used it was not at all romantic to me. But now that I think of it, he didn't compose poems to charm me. He saw the age difference and my white saree, an attire for widows, the day he knocked on my door.

The fact that he was not besotted by my ageing beauty was far less a problem though. Much like the sequins of fire, rumours also fly. A Muslim boy (almost man) living alone in the mansion of a Bengali widow was exactly what people loved to talk about over tea and spew dirt about.

Most of them were my husband's friends or acquaintances

and knew well that the mansion had fourteen rooms, seven on each side of the giant courtyard. For several years, I had served them tea and glucose biscuits in the centre of that courtyard. But that didn't stop them from concluding that I was sleeping with Shabbir.

A few nights, some drunk men had also knocked at my door, hoping for me to let them in. In their head, my town's men and women had already termed me a prostitute. But Shabbir was unfazed by all this. He hardly spoke, except for when he wanted an audience for his poems. He even took his bath away from the mansion, much to my disappointment.

After almost two months of living like this, something changed about him. On the radio, we would hear about the anticipated announcement of independence and partition that might happen any given day. The new prime minister of Britain, Clement Attlee from the Liberal Party, had fast-tracked the entire process. The 8 p.m. music programme on the radio was interrupted on a daily basis with some announcement or other by Lord Mountbatten, the viceroy. The only thing left to make known was the date.

This was a fairly political affair and so the date stayed tentative for a while. Very near to our place, for a little while, we heard that Gandhiji was supposed to come. He wanted to talk to people. Men, women, children. Old and young, Hindus and Muslims. Upper caste and lower caste. He wanted everyone to assemble in one single ground to listen to him.

'If we can't stand in one ground together, what is the point of independence?' Gandhi said during a radio interview.

But times were such that the crowd even overruled Gandhiji. He cancelled his address and returned to Calcutta. Things only became worse. People began killing people almost in a mundane way. Crowds turned into mobs, mobs into monsters.

They might have belonged to different sects, but all their faces looked the same. Satan had taken over India.

In Harsapur, Muslims were a minority. They soon started fleeing. Those who stayed formed their own mob. Shabbir became their leader. I would hear his poems being recited as slogans at night. I didn't see Shabbir after the night he led his mob for the first time. Honestly, I was scared. All these mobs, Hindus and Muslims, wanted to avenge something. What? No one cared to answer.

One day, a young man I knew knocked on my door.

'We have killed your lover.'

I stayed silent.

'He just murdered the temple priest.'

'Shabbir would never do that.'

'He just did.'

I couldn't argue.

'He is in a safe place now. But you need to stay shut about it. You are our own, the widow of our respected Deshbandhu Babu. We won't harm you. But he needed to die.'

I started running as soon as he disappeared. Maybe I could find him, at least dead. It was dark. I guessed my way to the next square. A group of men sat there around a bonfire. As I crossed them, one of them recognised me and whispered something to the others. They stood and stopped me.

'Don't go looking for him. He is right here.'

They pointed towards a gunny bag. They asked me to stay. I complied. My head had gone numb. Two of them opened the gunny bag and put it upside down. Hundreds of pieces of meat fell off into the fire. At the very end, they burned his clothes. I saw it all, silently. After a while, all of him was no more. They left me alone with the fire.

The next week, India and Pakistan celebrated independence.

There were speeches on both sides. They all talked about the future, about destiny, about pride. No one talked about Shabbir.

I sometimes wish I had a tangible picture of him which I could burn once and for all. But I don't. Instead, I see him in the smoke that rises from every fire in this world. At one hundred and two, my eyes are now tired. May this be the last fire I have to light. May this winter free me from my penance.

SPOON

BY NINO KHUNDADZE

He entered a new city. His next destination was reached without any problems with his bicycle. His last energy was spent in finding a nice spot to rest and look around. With the last of his money, he bought a piece of newly baked bread. He had arrived.

It was a nice evening; a chilly breeze blowing from the sea made him smile. It was especially pleasant after a long ride on a hot day. Now he could relax. He gave himself permission to enjoy the evening. He would take care of tomorrow, tomorrow. He could hear the pulsation of the sea mixed with sounds from the city accompanied by the thousand words coming from all over. He felt like he was in a theatre, watching a play from a comfortable seat, observing and enjoying. Here he was, having the whole world, becoming one with it, but seen as nothingness, receiving nothing from the eyes around him. He did not care, he was used to it, he was in his own world, celebrating that he could make it that far; it was hard, but he had done it.

Night is the most magical time of the day, he thought. When street lights come to life, all of the dirt and garbage of the day is transformed into sparkling gemstones. Magic is surrounding the whole city and reality disappears to somewhere else. That scene had made the play even more interesting, making the observer dive into the dim light. Suddenly, he saw a strange-shaped thing sparkling on the road, almost calling him. He followed the instinct and got it. It was an old spoon, smashed, flattened, but still somehow holding the grace of an old-fashioned piece from the past. Perfect for the theatre play it was found in. An idea had brightened up his mind. He rushed to the bicycle, got the bag full of tools, found the one he needed and started to shape his idea into physical reality. In a few minutes he was holding a nice ring folded from the spoon he had found. The next idea did not make him wait too long. He could sell it. This ring was tomorrow's bread.

Suddenly, he heard rushing footsteps behind his back; the sound of stepping on tools continued the music. A fall and a soft female voice full of tears ended the song. He ran to the woman. She was crying. He did not know what to do. He thought it was his fault, so he apologised a thousand times, while helping her to get up. Soon it was obvious he was not the reason for her tears. He tried to find out what was wrong, but it only made her cry more. The only words he could understand were: 'He lied to me, he lied to me.' His experienced mind figured out what was going on. He felt the cool ring of the spoon in his hands. He gave it to the woman, saying that it had brought him luck and now he was giving this precious creation to her. Her crying stopped. She was so surprised she did not know what to say or do. All she could observe was that her sadness was gone, disappeared, she did not care anymore. She had been seen, heard and understood by a stranger without even saying a word. Avoiding his face, she said 'Thank you,' the longest thank you he had ever heard.

STEP BY STEP

BY MARION HERMANNSEN

Nobody said anything the day I wore a sequinned shirt. The bartender winked at me, and one of the waitresses smiled. Of course, when I caught the night bus home, I was wearing a big jacket. One step at a time.

When I slipped the key into the lock on my flat door, I leaned my forehead against the peeling paint. The cool surface felt soothing against my sweaty skin. I was exhausted but too high to go to sleep straightaway. I pottered about for a little while, then pulled out my mobile.

I usually waited until I got to the safety of my own four walls before checking my messages. If there were unpleasant news, there was always my bed to hug and comfort me. Like tonight. Nina's disembodied voice sounded from the tinny speakers of my mobile.

'Braaand,'—why on earth she insisted on abbreviating my name Brandon was beyond me. 'Don't you dare stand me up tonight. If you're not here in ten minutes, we're over.'

My stomach dropped. I'd forgotten to cancel. Something else to deal with, but not tonight. I pulled my shirt over my head and sniffed it. My nose wrinkled. The faint whiff of sweat wafted from the fabric. I filled my bathroom sink with cold water and made sure the shirt was submerged. Then finally I fell into bed and was out like a light.

I was lying in bed, browsing to find some cute outfits online when somebody banged on the door. When I opened, Nina pushed past me, her face like thunder. I followed her meekly.

She was formidable when angry. Her fashionably long, straight hair swung around her head as if it were weighted at the ends. Her blue eyes glared at me out of a pretty face with makeup that was, as always, on point.

I wondered if she'd give me some tips but forgot about it when she opened her mouth. The way she said my name, 'Braaand,' sounded like a donkey's lovelorn cry for his mate. One of my colleagues had said that, and I couldn't disagree.

'Braaand, what's goin' on with ya lately? Don't ya want t'be with me no more?'

She shimmied over to me and put her arms around my neck. I didn't know what to say. How could I explain to her I didn't want to be with her—I wanted to be *like* her? One step at a time.

'I'm sorry, darling. It's not going to work out. It's not you, it's me. I'm being offered a promotion at work, and I won't have time to spend with you any longer.' I took a deep breath. There. That had sounded good, hadn't it?

Nina didn't seem to think so. She stepped back, and the glare was back with full force.

'That's the shittiest excuse I ever heard. You work at a fucking bar, Braaand.'

She sashayed to the door and slammed it as hard as she could. I should have been devastated. Instead, a weight lifted off my mind.

I hadn't had time to process what it meant to not be Nina's sidekick any more. No more demands for my time, no more justifying myself to her brawny Essex friends. No, I wouldn't hit the gym. No, I wouldn't eat more protein to bulk up.

I got on with my day, washed out the sequinned shirt, and got ready for work. The reception last night had been encouraging. Tonight, I'd wear another tight-fitting shirt from the women's section at the local boutique.

When I looked into my toilet mirror, the slight smile on my face surprised me. I was actually excited about this.

My shift ended before midnight. I washed my hands and paused. Next to the sink, one of the girls had left her makeup bag. Susie's, by the looks of it. I hesitated. I'd seen the girls swap makeup with each other, and the bag called to me. My hand shook when I peeked inside. Mascara, eyeliner, lipstick. Perfect.

Fifteen minutes later, I left the bar through the backdoor. The orange streetlights threw an eerie glow over the dark, wet road. There was no way I'd catch the night bus with full makeup on. So I walked, my head between my shoulder blades.

Every time I thought of the face staring back at me from the mirror less than an hour ago, I felt more excited. Like my true self was allowed to shine for once. I straightened my spine and walked more confidently. One step at a time.

That night I lay in bed, staring at the ceiling. Did I want to be a woman? Not really. But wearing pretty clothes and makeup? A smile pulled at the corners of my mouth. Being somebody else for a few hours other than scrawny loser Brandon. Shedding expectations, creating my own reality—the thought was as seductive as it was powerful.

When I showed up at work with eyeliner and a pretty blouse, the boss pulled me aside.

'Look, I appreciate you exploring your... feminine side, but can you do it somewhere else? We're not a trans club, you know. Our guests expect one or the other, not ... *this*.' Did he really have to gesture up and down in front of me to make his point?

And just like that, the tightness around my chest was back. The weight of the expectations on me. His gaze softened but his voice remained hard.

'Brandon, I have no idea what you're going through. Why don't you take some time off and think about what you want to do with your life? Come back when you've sorted yourself out, for fuck's sake.'

My shoulders drooped. I felt like a deflated balloon. I'd gone in high with excitement, and now my boss had stuck a pin into me. But he was right. I needed to sort my head out. My emotions were all over the place. Susie stopped me on the way to the door.

'You look so pretty, Brandon. Have you ever considered drag?'

My eyebrows shot to my hairline. Drag? Performing in front of people? Developing an alter-ego, much sassier than I could ever be? All the pieces fell into place under Susie's observant eyes.

'You like that, don't you? I always thought you'd be perfect for it. You can be such a bitch sometimes. No offence. The club my brother work at is always looking for class acts. If you're up for it, I'll sort out an interview for you. You'd start as server, but they'll help you develop your act.'

I laughed, my chest widening with each exhale. Drag. Seriously? My life was about to take a left turn, but damn, was I excited.

STORY OF A PIXEL

BY YOUSIF SHAMSA

The pixel got a command to light grey. The neighbouring pixels were other shades of grey. The one to the left was a bit lighter. The one to the right was a bit darker. For the observer, the pixels formed a continuum. All pixels worked together. But our pixel longed for more. He longed for a solo performance. Being just another pixel sickened him. What about me? What is my goal in life? What is there next for me? He reflected on his dreams when he grew up. He always dreamed of travelling, discovering the world.

The pixel received a new command. Grey again. *I can't do this anymore.* Still, he turned his colour to grey while thinking of his potential. To take other colours. To be green, blue, red. To be all kinds of combinations of green, blue and red. But not grey. *For God's sake not grey.* A new command. Lighter grey. Darker grey. Lighter grey. Darker grey. *I can't do it. I just can't.* And then it happened. The pixel lit up with all colours at once, despite the command grey. The observer stood up. Walked to the display. Examined it carefully.

'Damn! A dead pixel!'

TEETH

BY LIDIA GALLI

It's hot and I'm sweating like a pig, but we're on a job and I have to sit around in this van for a little longer. From the window, a beige and brown landscape welcomes me. I'd love to go to the island of Ortigia, walk around in its labyrinth of ancient streets until reaching the little church I went to as a child, and rest breathing the fresh air; or leave everything behind, drive to the sea and just jump in its cool waters, but I can't. A sweltering Sicilian summer is the worst period to do this kind of job. My insides burn as if the sun itself could reach them, I can smell my skin slowly heating up, and the stench coming from the melting asphalt. I yawn. We've been here an hour already. It's all the Dwarf's fault, always imploring us to head out early. Well, he's the one paying the higher price: he's standing under the sun next to the courthouse with his filthy cigarettes, drowning in his own sweat. My reflection in the rearview mirror catches my eye. The sweat trickles from underneath my thinning black hair. I'm 32 and almost bald, but in Siracusa it's a blessing. Midday's the worst hour during summer, but it's also the quietest one. I open my mouth and check my incisors, canines and premolars. Teeth have always been fascinating for me. Adult teeth, that is, the ones you will use for the rest of your life, at least until some lowlife knocks them out of your mouth in a brawl. Animals kill with their teeth, but only to eat or to survive. Men, on the other hand, do it for power, money, and sometimes even for love. The deadliest men are those who have tasted a little bit of wealth; they are always brutal, ruthless, ready to fight to keep what they have. In this sense, we're all innocent. Crimes are the fault of our own perverse nature. We're white souls in a shit-world. As for me, I don't smoke, I don't drink and I don't chase down other women. I want to provide for my family, and it just so happens that I enjoy this line of work.

My friends know of my interest in teeth. They call me the Dentist. Behind my back they joke about it, but never to my face. They know better. I like my nickname, though; in this field we all get one. I work with the Dwarf, the shortest and the most low-profile of us; the Tank, more mountain than man; the Hammer, talented with tools of every kind; and the Alien, a sneaky guy with big dark eyes. We never use our true names, especially over the phone, as someone's bound to be eavesdropping. My job makes my family life hard; my wife doesn't want our son to follow in my footsteps, and she's always worried sick for us both. Every day on the job could be my last, but I don't care. The boss will take care of my family if something happens to me, like if I'm ever caught, it's the golden rule. But for my boy... I would like a better future for him. Two weeks ago I asked to the boss not to force him to work in our field too, to allow him to leave to study in Rome when he's older. I had just finished an incredible job, and he was quite impressed by my decision taking. The boss said he would think about it. I'm the best man he's got, and loyal to a fault; it could be very beneficial for his business – he could ask anything of me if he promised to leave my son out of this. Last week my wife Sandra and I had a big fight about our boy's future, and I told her of my request to the boss; she sobbed out of sheer joy and hope. We're like a newly-wed couple with all the attention she gives me now. The only problem left between me and Sandra is my ever-growing teeth collection. She finds it disgusting, but she knows better than to ask me where I find them. Our son, on the other hand, loves to look at them with me and asks me every day if I have any new teeth to show him. Maybe this will lead to him becoming an actual dentist one day.

A sudden noise snaps me out of it. The Dwarf is blowing his nose so loudly he's doubled over with the effort. The signal. A middle-aged man with an elegant shirt and black trousers comes out from the courthouse. The snitch, the scumbag that sent the boss's brother to jail. I smile, thinking of the special bath the Tank is already preparing for him. My life becomes a movie in slow motion: the Hammer opens the *Ducato* door for me. I don't hear what he's saying, I don't care. In two seconds I am already behind my prey, my hands around his neck, feeling his vain attempts to breathe, strangling him just until he goes to sleep. He doesn't deserve to die so easily. I will decide how his end will be. Maybe I will let him take the bath alive; oh yes, that will teach him a lesson. On a day like this, I love my job. We are a precise and deadly machine, my friends and I. For them it has become a routine job: take, kill, destroy the body. For me, it's still thrilling. I'm the one always volunteering to clean the bathtub afterwards. The mask can't hold back the stench of death and chemicals, especially on a hot day like this, but I don't care. At the bottom of the acid bath, among the few human remains left, I always find my treasure: new teeth for my collection.

THE BRIEF CHRONICLER
BY CHRISTOPHER MORAHAN

He cupped his hands around the cigarette and lighter to protect the flame from the falling rain. Standing in the doorway of the fire exit, he leafed absentmindedly through the programme that he had picked up backstage. Smoking his first cigarette in over three months, he glanced at some black-and-white photographs of the production – including a particularly tired and wrinkled one of him – a few advertisements and an interview with the director. On the centre page he found the list of cast members. He stared at the second name in the billing: Benjamin MacDonald. The opposite page consisted of just a single sentence, printed in bold white letters against a black background. *To be, or not to be, that is the question.*

Or so it had been, once upon a time. It was a question he himself had asked on many stages and of many audiences in London and further afield. But now, after so many years, the question had changed. Now it was simply, 'To the left, or to the right?'

To the right: the adoring crowd. They were there tonight, as they were every night, waiting to ask for autographs and to take selfies with the stars of the show. While audience members no longer greeted him with the same kind of enthusiasm they once did, it had, nonetheless, remained part of a ritual for him. It reminded him of a time when he still needed the attention.

And on the other hand, to the left: the lonely walk to the Tube station. The lonely walk home.

He leaned out of the doorway and looked to his right. In the distance he could see John Jeffries, the Hamlet to his Claudius, making small talk with some fans. He took another drag of his cigarette. It was still raining. He would wait for the rain to clear first. He still had time to decide.

Adoring crowd. It was a phrase that he heard so often, but was there really any truth to it? Do ordinary people truly *adore* celebrities? Or was it simply a game they all played? *You massage my ego and I give you a souvenir to take back home to show your friends and family.* It was a game he had played for decades, but lately with less success than he had been used to.

When was the last time he had been given a leading role in anything? Would he ever see his name at the top of any billing again? His time had ended before he even realised it. Other actors had taken his place. Younger, better-looking, more charismatic, more witty. More loved. More *adored*. And once upon a time, he had been one of them.

Several nights earlier he had tried to bring up the subject with the actress who played opposite him as Gertrude. 'It happens to us all, darling,' she simply said. 'We each strut and fret our hour on the stage. But an hour is all we get. You have to make it count.' Of course, she was still younger than him. She still had time.

'Mr MacDonald, I'm afraid we have to keep the fire escape clear.'

He turned around to face the usher who had addressed him, then turned around again to stare out onto the street.

'I'm sorry,' the usher added, still standing behind him. 'Health and Safety.'

That was another thing that had changed. There had been a time when he could have smoked a cigarette out here in peace and no one would have dreamed of bothering him. Fine. The rain was starting to clear up anyway. *It's time to stop feeling so sorry for yourself.*

'By the way, great show tonight!'

MacDonald turned around once more to face the usher, but the latter had already disappeared around the corner before he could think of anything to say in reply. Instead, he faced out onto the street once more and took one last drag from his cigarette.

The day was soon coming that he would have to turn left. But it wasn't tonight. He tossed his cigarette to the ground and stepped out onto the pavement. Walking over to the crowd of people huddling under their umbrellas, he could see that Jeffries was already gone. Or at least he couldn't see him. Just Gertrude and Ophelia. He smiled for photographs and signed autographs, always casting the occasional sideways glance to count the number of fans mobbing his co-stars. It reminded him of a time when he still needed the attention.

THE FIRST DAY

BY NINO KHUNDADZE

The start of her week was usual. It was Monday, the first day of a month, early morning. She took a nice relaxing walk through the empty streets. Destination: the grey building of her office was reached too soon, or wonderful weather made her feel that way. She entered the office and the total peacefulness outside was replaced with chaos and hysteria. The voices were so mixing up that she could not understand a word. She saw Max and asked him the reason. He just pointed to the information board with a confused face.

The board was totally blank but for one note in huge writing. It said that from the next month salaries would be regulated with new rules. Each and every one of them would get only smiles, as many as they could earn. If someone did not like it, they were free to leave.

She could not believe her eyes. Thousands of thoughts overloaded her mind. What would she do? She could not feed her children or pay the rent with smiles. For a moment the world stopped and she was lost in her thoughts. An alarm, like music, woke her mind up to reality. The music ended and a voice, very familiar to all, her boss, said: *Happy April the first.*

THE MOONLIGHT ON A THURSDAY
BY JULIE SHERIDAN

Isaac Baird likes the stature of a bar stool. After work on a Thursday, his favourite spot is just right of the entrance, slightly in the shadows, with a line of sight on the giant screen over the bar. At the Moonlight Inn, they play music videos on loop and Isaac sits sipping his beer and pretends he's watching them. Most of the time, though, he's watching people. Young people, old people, drunk people, sober people, loose-lipped people, lock-lipped people. He watches them all.

What is it brings them to the Moonlight Inn tonight? The people who appear to have found happiness are here for lovers or for family or to share a regular drink with friends. Their laughter and banter and the casual audacity of their physical interactions beguiles him. These happy people wear their contentment like a comfortable armour shielding them from all the cruelty of the world. The others – the ones still looking for happiness – all appear to be searching for it in the same hopeless places: at the bottom of another glass of malt or with a random, nameless hook-up in the parking lot or in a restroom stall. Isaac came to the conclusion several Thursday nights ago that there are only two types of people who frequent the Moonlight Inn: the well-balanced types and the slightly unhinged types. And he isn't quite sure which type he is yet. Maybe he's an individual. But he doubts it. He stopped believing in individuals back when he joined the army. He hears the door creak to his left, adjusts himself on his stool and side-eyes her as she enters the bar. She's busy removing sunglasses and folding them into a case so she doesn't even notice him noticing her as she glides by.

Vivienne Stewart loathes the indignity of a bar stool. Its clunky woodenness calls to mind the highchairs of infancy: babies drooling and snotting, slurring cryptic sounds, ultimately helpless, like drunks at closing time. Vivienne hoists herself up, straddles the stool, then tries her best to arrange her legs comfortably. She busies herself fixing her collar and rearranging the sleeves of her cashmere cardigan, all the while scanning her surroundings. The name *Moonlight Inn* hadn't quite conjured up this vision of humdrum. When she'd made the date, she'd imagined shades of dark blue: petrol and midnight and peacock. A touch of gold here, some silver there, stars and tea lights and mirrored mosaics. This place is nothing like she pictured. It's generic. It's derivative. It's any bar, any city, any country. A heavily-scented waitress comes to the table and busies herself wiping it, although it is already perfectly clean. The name tag pinned to her small but stacked bosom reads *Olympia*. Underneath, in italics, it reads *According to Chemistry, Alcohol is a Solution!* The waitress rolls her eyes.

'The owner, Karl, he thinks he's a comic genius.' She says it out of the side of her mouth, playfully conspiratorial.

An image of a sweaty fat man wearing a novelty tie flashes into Vivienne's head. She smiles at the waitress. 'Your *name* caught my eye,' she says, oddly comfortable in this tiny girl-woman's presence. 'It's very unusual.'

Another eye roll. '*Steel Magnolias* was like *every*one's favourite movie the year I was born. There were like three Shelbys and two Annelles in my high school year. But my Mom just *loved* Ms Clairee so she called me after that actress... Olympia...'

'...Dukakis,' Vivienne says. As the name passes her lips, her mind conjures up another image of television news and a little presidential candidate perched high on an army tank. It's on that temperamental box TV that she and Emilia had the whole time they lived in Harrisburg. The memory warms her on the inside. Vivienne is aware now that the waitress, Olympia, is looking at her, waiting for an answer.

'Oh, I'm sorry. My mind wandered a little. What did you say?'

'That's okay,' Olympia says. 'Mine does that too. Only way to get through the day, sometimes!' She laughs, nudging Vivienne lightly. 'I was just asking if I could get you anything.'

Instinctively, Vivienne checks her watch. She got here fifteen minutes early by design and reckons it will be at least another ten before Emilia and Mia arrive. She looks up, catches sight of a man bringing a bottle of beer to his lips. 'Just a Miller, please.' She sees the waitress raise a slight eyebrow. She has surprised herself too. But beer, mass-produced and bland, seems to fit this place.

Olympia nudges a bar stool with her hip and moves it out of her way. She carries glasses stacked high, gripping them between her chin and shoulder. She feels Isaac Baird's eyes on her as she moves by him. She's used to men's eyes following her. But she likes it when it's Isaac. He doesn't say much but Olympia knows he is a gentleman. She just knows.

Karl is *not* a gentleman. He thinks he can take liberties

because he owns the place. Karl has positioned himself at the narrowest point of the bar so she has to rub against him as she squeezes by. She hears what he's going to say before he says it. 'Easy, Olympia, honey. There's *laws* against that kind of touching.' Donnie Whitehead, who's propping up the bar, laughs toothlessly into his pitcher of beer. A joke is nothing without an audience. Olympia knows that. But even Karl must be getting tired of the same old material. He makes wisecracks about *her* sexually harassing *him* about three times every shift. Olympia knows his game. Attack is the best form of defence. She takes a bottle of Miller from the fridge and uncaps it. She fills a bowl with pretzels and places it on her tray beside the Miller and moves to squeeze past Karl again. He doesn't say anything but Donnie snorts so she figures the joke is some kind of a hand gesture. Karl has many hand gestures. *It's a shame he hasn't as many brain cells,* Olympia thinks and smiles as she delivers the beer to the wistful lady sitting by the restroom.

The lady is way too classy for the Moonlight Inn. Olympia notes the chunky amber necklace, the soft blue knitwear and the embroidered slipper shoes. Olympia guesses that she is educated and creative, serene but not settled. Even though there's a thin gold band on her ring finger, she doesn't strike Olympia as wife material. She looks like she takes care of herself just for herself. Olympia realises that she's starting to think up a life story for this lady. Olympia often thinks up stories to distract herself from Karl's jibes. She doesn't write them down. Maybe she should.

She looks over at Isaac and he raises his beer bottle and smiles his shy smile. She gives him a thumbs up and heads to the bar to get him another Miller. When she returns, she squeezes his upper arm gently as she replaces the empty bottle with the new one. She feels the smooth curve of his bicep. She likes that he takes care of himself. He smells good too. Olympia doesn't say anything because she knows Isaac isn't a big talker. She is happy just knowing that the silent communication between them is something real.

Isaac doesn't know what it is about this woman that he finds so... *arresting* is the word that comes to mind. It is a word he would choose not to speak: too much sibilance. He darts another look at her, examining her as she toys with the strap of her watch. He cannot decide how old she is but he knows she is older than him. Her hair is a light shade of brown and her skin is smooth and taut, gleaming like the polished porcelain of his sister Stacey's cherished Lladro figurine. *Someday*, he remembers telling Stacey, *I'm going to get you another Lladro – straight from the factory in Spain*. It's a memory from what could have been another life, back when Isaac wanted to flee to Spain and stay there. He still loves the lisping sound of Spanish.

The video for TLC's *Waterfalls* plays on the big screen and Isaac looks at it intently. He remembers this video. He remembers the words to the song. He even remembers that Lisa 'Left Eye' Lopes from TLC set fire to her boyfriend's sneakers in a bathtub. He doesn't remember who her boyfriend was. Isaac smiles inside when he thinks about afternoons watching MTV with his sister, back when it was just the two of them.

Isaac's eyes drop to look at the woman again. She takes a sip from her beer and stares into the space ahead of her. He thinks she is thinking, but she doesn't smile or frown, so they must be easy thoughts. Isaac would like to be the one she is having easy thoughts about.

Vivienne checks her watch again. Her daughter will be here soon. The life Emilia has chosen does not sit easy with her. She takes a long, slow slug from the beer bottle, then wipes her mouth with the back of her hand. It feels good to do something so boorish. Vivienne thinks in that instant that her life has perhaps become too refined. Vivienne is comfortable with refinement. She calls the waitress over.

'Could I get a sparkling water with a twist of lime?' she asks, 'please.'

'Sure thing,' the waitress says, grabbing the empty beer bottle by the neck. Vivienne notices the tininess of her wrists, the fraying friendship bracelet with a silver star, the semi-colon tattoo. She guesses the girl is about twenty but then remembers their exchange about *Steel Magnolias* and realises she's closer to thirty. Emilia is thirty-five now and Mia is almost thirteen. She still thinks of her granddaughter as a child of five, full of giggles and honest observations, untouched by the harshness of the adult world. Sometimes she thinks of Emilia like this too, but realises that she was never that child. Emilia always had something to prove. Even now, with four children at home and a husband with a handsome salary who has already paid off their five-bed McMansion, Emilia still works fifty-hour weeks and goes on five business trips a month. The youngest of the children is only three, so it's not like Emilia isn't needed elsewhere. But you can't say these things to Emilia. These days, you can't say them to *anyone*. The mere suggestion of a more traditional lifestyle choice is perceived as a body blow to the eternal fight for women's rights. But then who is she to talk about more traditional lifestyle choices? Vivienne smiles at the thought.

Olympia catches the lady covering a smile with her hand. It's like a cloud covering the sunshine. 'Smiles are for sharing,' she says to the lady as she places the glass down beside her. It's out of her mouth before she even realises she's said it. Olympia sees the surprise register on the lady's face and is about to apologise when the lady smiles again. It is like standing in the warm glow of sunshine after two days of rain. 'That is the wisest observation I've heard in a long time,' Vivienne says. She means it. It feels like a lifetime since she's heard anyone say something so real.

Isaac notices Olympia sharing a joke with the woman for a second time. He likes how Olympia knows how to treat people. Even when she doesn't say a word, she is kind. *A nice piece of ass* is what Isaac's brother-in-law Teddy calls Olympia. He deliberately places emphasis on the *S* sounds in *nice*, *piece* and *ass*. It's a lazy taunt, one that Isaac barely hears any more. Teddy thinks Olympia is the reason Isaac drinks at the Moonlight Inn. Teddy is the reason Isaac drinks at the Moonlight Inn. Teddy gets home early on Thursdays, infecting the household with his malcontent. Isaac thinks drinking beers and watching people is a healthier option than enduring his brother-in-law. Any port in a storm. The door creaks again and Isaac looks up to see a smart young businesswoman parade by with an older man stepping furtively behind her. There is a similarity in their features. He guesses that they are daughter and father. He turns his head slightly to the right and risks another look at the woman. She is circling ice cubes around a highball glass. She looks up and her eyes meet his. It is only for a second or two but, for Isaac, time stands still. He feels her grace, her integrity, her grit. She reminds him of a deer that has been startled by a sudden noise or movement. He hopes that she feels something too. The businesswoman and her father obscure his view of her. He curses them under his breath. That one sublime moment is shattered into a thousand pieces of nothing.

Vivienne is still thinking about Emilia. She wonders if her daughter is as she is because there wasn't a man around to provide mannish things, ideas, influences. In her late teens, Emilia's means of rebelling was to work doggedly towards landing a husband. She succeeded and married Bradley on her twenty-first birthday. She has been working to get away from him ever since. Vivienne takes a sip of her drink, then swirls the ice cubes in the water, enjoying the tinkle as ice meets glass. She looks over towards the door, waiting. Her eyes stop for a moment as they meet those of a clean-cut young man sitting in the shadows. In that moment she feels his singularity, his brittleness, his want. He reminds her of a dog cowering from a thunderstorm. She looks away and notices that Emilia is walking towards her. Emilia is not accompanied by Mia. Emilia is accompanied by a memory.

Olympia senses the tension as she approaches the table to take their order. The woman is sitting ramrod straight and there's a muscle flickering in her neck. Her eyes are locked wide as she looks across the table at the fancily dressed young woman. The man sitting with them has the same slanting nose and jutting cheekbones as the younger woman. The two women have the exact same eyes: perfect ovals of turquoise blue like swimming pools seen from the sky.

Olympia knows the young woman's type. She asks for a Semillon Blanc, pronouncing the name of the wine in a French accent. It is perhaps the first time someone has asked for a Semillon Blanc here. It is definitely the first time someone has pronounced it properly. Olympia remembers she once asked Karl about wine. He said *Here at the Moonlight, we serve two superlative varieties of wine: red and white.* She has since learned that the white they serve is a Chardonnay. When she tells the young woman this, she responds with a sigh and 'Well, I guess that will have to do, then.' The young woman calls the other woman *Mom* as she asks if she wants another drink. The woman shakes her head. She asks the man what he'll drink but she does not call him *Dad*. She calls him *Raymond*. He orders a Tom Collins. He looks like a man who knows how to drink. Olympia recognises it in the redness of his nose and the dark pillows of his eyes. She has known many men who know how to drink. Olympia leaves the table but she is still close enough to hear it when the younger woman says, 'I don't know why you're so shocked, Mom. You must have known I'd want to find him.'

Isaac picks at the label on his beer bottle. He does not want to look at her any more. He has seen enough stilted conversations between ageing couples and their grown up children. He sees them most Thursdays when he sits in his favourite spot, just right of the entrance and slightly in the shadows. Isaac doesn't want this to be just another one of those Thursdays. He wants to live forever in the warmth of that moment when his eyes met hers. He wants to imagine how he would treat this woman better, please her better, love her better. He does not want to feel this, the familiar realisation that something extraordinary has become as mediocre as his choice of beer.

Isaac Baird climbs down from his barstool. He slips his arms into the sleeves of his jacket, thinking of all the things he might have said to the woman. He might let these thoughts soar above him for a while. But his feet are back on the ground.

THE PLAY

BY MARTINA LACKNER

Mike had been performing for a couple of years. Becoming a completely different person, pretending to be *not himself* – it fascinated him. To be a super-rich old playboy or a sophisticated intellectual, it was just his *thing*. Of course his costumes were always perfectly customised to his roles. Being a tall, handsome guy in his early thirties, it was easy for him to slip into different characters.

Mike was a person who did not care about other people. He cared for animals, though. He gave up eating meat when he was twelve. When he turned seventeen, his theatre friends convinced him to become vegan. So, for more than half of his life, he hadn't eaten any animal products. And he liked it that way. Being a vegan gave him the feeling of being superior to the rest of the crowd. Despite being on stage in the theatre, Mike believed that his veganism was a fundamental element of his extraordinariness: he was a chosen one. He did not feel at all ashamed to treat his company condescendingly. In fact, he believed that it was his duty to do so, to teach people 'a lesson.' It was because of this that, a couple of years ago, he and his friends started to pick people they perceived as not fitting into society.

Their ultimate goal was to make them realise that they did not fit. Mike and his friends pretended to be kind. On cordial terms, they would gain these people's trust just to show them in the most subtle ways possible what they were: on the verges of American society. After his plays, Mike always felt very complacent. In the end it was also kind of practice for his acts on stage. Like his favourite children's book hero – Lucky Luke – once he was done, he usually lit a cigarette and drove on his black horse (a Harley Davidson Street 500) off towards the sun. Or rather, towards his favourite vegan, gluten-free restaurant in Denver.

But his self-confidence decomposed with his last play. Mike used to be found in Denver's bookstores for his plays. Now, it was cosy to find a new 'target' there. After all, which normal person would spend a lot of money on books? Only insecure, anxious people looked for answers to their lives in boring books. There were also the nerds, the lunatics and the do-gooders. He detested all of them from the very bottom of his heart. So, he would just sit in the bookstore's cafeteria and wait. After a short period of time, the door opened a window of opportunity: a tall, skinny, black woman in her late twenties entered. Her hair was shoulder-length and curly. It was not arranged, but looked kind of wild. Her posture was straight – elegant and elevated. Before she entered it fully, she observed the bookstore. His first thought was: *This is an easy and appropriate target!* She looked well-educated, she looked conceited, she looked like she was fortunate. And how dare she? Her place in society was not at the top but at the bottom. It was his task to teach her this lesson.

Mike stood up, stretched his back to reveal his full size to her and his imaginary audience. She should see what real sophistication meant. Mike was the incarnation of sophistication. He walked slowly towards her. The woman was standing in front of the bookshelves radiating a kind of serenity which almost made him stop for one second. But no, the closer Mike came, the more her true nature revealed itself to him: she was a timid, fearful woman who gave the impression of being a girl rather than a woman. The closer he came, the more he scanned the books in the bookshelf in front of her. It was the feminist section. Mike's fingers became a clenched fist. He smiled but it was fake. It was a forced smile. Only two metres separated them. Mike ran his fingers over the titles on the back of the books and made one side-step to come closer to her. There was almost no-one around them. He stopped when he was an arm's length away from her and glanced to the book she was holding: the sub-title was *The Logic of Misogyny*. This gave him one hundred percent certainty and permission: she really *needed* to be taught. He relaxed his hands and lips, took a deep breath and approached her.

'Listening to the latest news about Trump... isn't this book of great relevance?' Her glance suggested she was puzzled. It was followed by a few seconds of silence.

'What do you mean?'

'I mean, isn't Trump the living proof that misogyny exists?'

Her glance still was puzzled though changing to a certain kind of hesitance. Silence, again. Does she really need more explanation? The seconds passed but felt like minutes before finally she said: 'Yeah, you are right... sorry... I need to go!'

Without waiting for his reply, she put the book back on the shelf, turned around and left. She almost ran outside. Now, it was Mike who was puzzled. It had never happened to him before that his charm and cordialness didn't work on his target. After all, didn't everyone seek a nice fellow to release them from their solitude? How dare she leave him before he had even started his game? It drove him nuts.

If Mike started a game, he had to finish it. Mike wrote a note: *We met, it was raining and something about Trump really upset you. You are African-American and very beautiful. Meet me here next week, same time. M.* He folded the note, gave it to the bookstore seller. He told him to hand it to the woman next time she was there. This play was not over. He would get back to her and debase her. Mike stormed out of the bookstore. After such a failure, Mike could not drive off on his motorbike. He covered himself with a hoodie and walked home.

THE SONG

BY EKATERINA NOVGORODTSEVA

The cold had become the very fabric of existence, but Frigga still winced when the piercing wind greeted her outside. It felt like it ripped off the small stripe of skin that was showing between the scarf and goggles.

The generator rumbled a few steps outside the tent. It had gone out two times yesterday alone, when the oil inside had frozen. They had to make a fire to thaw it out again. Thank God they had enough fuel for that. But the fuel would run out in three days. The starship was supposed to come pick them up in two.

Frigga passed other tents, whose inhabitants huddled inside. They had all foregone the relative warmth of the caves to take part in one of the last mass evacuations. They burned through ungodly amounts of fuel to achieve a semblance of warmth in their makeshift tents. No one dared to miss the ship's arrival.

She walked awkwardly through the deep snow. Every step had to be taken carefully. The leg prosthesis still felt weird, despite months of use.

The short journey to the cliffs took much out of her. Exhausted and cold, Frigga wondered again about the point of it all. Nonetheless, she took out the violin and began tuning it. She hoped the instrument would last long enough in this vicious cold.

Frigga set the violin against her shoulder and paused. The ocean looked tranquil, but Frigga did not share the feeling. With something like desperation, Frigga plunged into the music. She had not played the violin since the flesh of her left arm had been replaced by metal.

It sounded dreadful at first. The mechanical arm failed to understand what the brain wanted of it. But this song had to be released before it was too late. And so Frigga played, despite the fear that the music would come out as mutilated as her body was. The jagged and tortured sounds that emerged slowly began to assemble into something like music. Frigga let the notes that she had memorised run from her hands.

Was this to be the last song played on this dying world? Frigga did not want to believe this to be true. But how many were left? Two more ships were transporting humans to the Outer Ring. Theirs was going to be the second last. Would the final humans on Earth find time to sing their goodbye? Frigga did not think so. Therefore, the duty fell to her.

Frigga blinked away the tears and furiously played her song. This was a song for the dead or the dying. Frigga's sister helped compose it. She belonged to the first category by the time Frigga lost the left arm.

A thunderous crack sounded. An iceberg, majestic and unstoppable, split from the middle and slid into the ocean. This was Frigga's audience. The ocean, the wind and the ice. This world was so beautiful, Frigga thought she'd cut her eyes on its merciless face.

Her right hand was getting tired. The mechanical joints of the left arm were resisting as the oil began thickening in the cold. Frigga had to fight to continue playing and was rewarded by someone joining her. A low moaning sound slowly filled the air. Frigga halted, listening. Then, a few hundred metres away, she saw a huge black body emerge from the water. It was a whale, the first one that Frigga had seen in her life. It turned to show a glistening red eye. There were bumps on the whale's skin. It looked sick, but Frigga knew that only its mutations kept it alive. It gave the whale the warmth necessary to survive, while the world around it died.

Despite the shaking of her hand, Frigga returned to playing the violin. She wasn't certain who was singing to whom – the whale to her or she to the whale? They were connected, as only two living beings among death could be. Frigga could no longer stop the tears.

The long sharp wails of the violin and the crescendo that followed were accompanied by the deep voice of the whale. Frigga wanted to believe that in some way the whale understood the song. It was defiance of death. Should not every living being understand it? Every ant and every tree? Every fish and every monkey?

A violin string snapped, almost striking her across the face. Frigga stopped playing, stunned by the interruption. She had to take off her goggles to wipe away the tears. The song was over. Interrupted by the indifferent cold, smothering the song just as the world was being smothered in snow.

It was time to leave.

But Frigga stood there for a few more minutes, even as she trembled with cold, and knew that lingering might mean her death. She watched the whale turn and erupt a water fountain before submerging to the depths again. It would live on for a few more years. If the hunger didn't kill it, the ice would. More and more of the ocean surface was freezing solid. One day, the whale would rise and helplessly beat against the ice prison. It would suffocate, encased in an icy tomb together with the rest of the world. But until then, it would sing. It would sing as Frigga's violin did. The whale would call for other souls and wait for their answer. It would be the world's final lullaby, but to Frigga it was something more. It was a reminder that before death, comes life. Before silence, comes song. This truth was irrevocable. This truth would not meet oblivion.

Frigga turned away from the bitter ocean and the empty sky. She had to live. She had to carry the song to the stars.

THE TEST

BY KRYSTA BROWN

She was screwing it up, badly. Her first exam at the CIA academy, and Amy was sinking fast. The instructor's voice in her earpiece, cool and judging, only made things worse. She struggled to focus on the task at hand, knowing he was watching her every move behind the tinted glass of the observation room, marking every mistake in his tablet. The irony was she felt she had been preparing for this test her entire life. If one could ever prepare for the Agency equivalent of jumping into an open shark cage at feeding time.

In her days at private school and university, she had spent long nights studying Hebrew and Mandarin and had picked up a working knowledge of Russian in the last few years, which her academy friends generously hinted she should brush up on before the test. Despite this, she had fumbled pathetically through the first task, taking way too much time to translate the hidden files from the cracked safe from Hebrew into English. Once she had, however, the message revealed the location of yet another stack of papers, folded into the pages of a book in the immense library on the far side of the examination office. Leo

Tolstoy's *War and Peace,* naturally in its original Russian. She started to sweat.

She knew the exam was designed to test her thought processes and decision-making skills as well as analyse her reactions to the various challenges. She could only assume breaking out in a cold sweat was not a desirable response to the current stimuli. She took a deep breath and glanced at the device on her wrist. It looked like a normal digital fitness watch, but it was monitoring more than just her heart rate. It was sampling the chemical composition of her sweat and analysing whatever hormones she was radiating into the room. The device linked to a program on her instructor's tablet called H.A.R.T., for Humanoid Algorithmic Response Tool, and it was probably having a field day monitoring her current freakout. She tried to lock her eyes onto the letters in her hand, each one written in a different language. Urdu, ancient Sanskrit, Old German – she didn't even know where to begin. Then she noticed that each letter was marked with a red number in the lower right page corner. That couldn't be coincidence. She checked Tolstoy's novel again, thinking she may have missed another clue. A flash of red caught her eye as she turned a page. The page number 6 was circled in the same red pen as the letter. It must be a match for the sixth letter! She flipped through the stack, pulling out a piece of yellowed stationery with Mandarin lettering and a red six in the corner. A few more times comparing the circled numbers in the book with the letters, and she had the combination 6, 3, 12, 7 and 9 in Mandarin, Russian, Old English, High German and, presumably, Icelandic. She took a closer look at the letters themselves, certain they held an important clue, though she had no idea what that could be. Surely they didn't expect her to read all this? Again, her eyes caught a tiny flash of red springing up from a page – this time, the letter 'a' had been written in red in part of a German word. She checked the other letters. Sure enough, the red letters in the other pages revealed the anagram 'makroshayt' – even from the Chinese she translated the character 'ma' into its Roman pinyin spelling. But now she was stuck.

'You're running out of time, cadet,' a chilling voice suddenly cut into her thoughts. 'Why don't you just call it quits and be done with it?'

She could feel a wave of indignation welling up, threatening to implode inside her. No doubt the H.A.R.T. was capturing that emotional nuance as well, she thought bitterly. She wanted to kick herself, feeling the sudden burning sensation of an anger she could not express in words – anger at him and his infuriatingly mocking voice, at her parents for encouraging her to pursue a career in the CIA, but mostly, she hated to admit, at herself. For being stupid enough to think she could hack it in the intelligentsia. She struggled to keep her emotions in check by imagining them being tucked away neatly in boxes, one inside the other, until she could not feel them anymore.

All of a sudden, it hit her. *Matryoshka!* Her gaze darted frantically around the room. There! She spotted the Russian nesting doll on the mantle behind the desk. She rushed over, nearly tripping over her own feet in a clumsy attempt at agility. She grabbed the doll, her entire attention focused on prying open the secret contained within.

Bang! A blast from the right tore into her side, sending pain searing through her in shockwaves. Too late, she realised she had failed to consider the possibility that a double-agent was still in the building with her. A fatal mistake. She knew then that she had failed. She could see the dark red fluid oozing from the outside of her jacket, dripping to form a pool of thick scarlet on the hardwood floor. And though she knew, somewhere in her rational mind, the blood was fake, she felt her eyes roll back into her head, her body breaking into a cold sweat. The last thing she saw was the floor rising up to meet her.

When she finally came to, she found herself looking up at the blank, unsmiling faces of the fake double-agent who had shot her and her instructor.

'Glad to see you could join us, cadet,' the instructor's lips formed a condescending sneer.

'I... I hate the sight of blood,' Amy stammered, feeling weak and pathetic.

The two men exchanged glances.

'Don't take this badly, kid,' the double-agent said, not unkindly. 'But I think assassin might be the wrong career for you.'

THE UNHAPPY ABACUS
BY MARTIN GAMBLE

The Abacus was moaning to the empty classroom again.

'I don't count anymore,' he said. 'I feel useless.' As he spoke, his coloured beads flicked from side to side along the metal rods that formed his torso. The beads made a clicking sound that created a mathematical fluidity to his speech. On the top of his head was a black toupee that contrasted with his grey and bushy moustache and eyebrows.

'How many years have you been sitting here?' asked a voice from the darkness.

'Too many to count!' he coughed. He had lost count of the number of times that he had lost count. 'The children can't even reach me because the shelf is too high.'

'What are you counting now?' asked the voice.

'I count everything,' replied the Abacus, emphatically. 'The number of odd pumps in the shoe box. The number of half-eaten crayons. The grains of sand in the sand box.' He paused. A few more beads flicked across his torso. 'And I count the Moon.' He smiled. The Abacus tilted his head and the toupee slipped a little to the side.

'How do you count the Moon?' continued the voice. The voice sounded soothing and teacher-like.

'I count her minutes and seconds in the sky. I count her cycles. And I count the beams of light that she shines through the windows at us.'

'And what do you count when the children are here?' asked the voice.

The Abacus scoffed. 'Ask The Calculator, it's his fault that I don't count with them anymore. With his fancy buttons and screen and solar panel. He might be faster than me, but I have colour. And I am the original!'

The Abacus clanked his walking stick down onto the shelf's floor. The noise sent an echo of tension across the room. Even the Moon looked over her shoulder to see where the noise had come from.

The Abacus tried to follow the sound of the voice and asked, 'Are you hiding in the stock cupboard?' The voice did not reply. His attention was distracted when he noticed a movement from the Hamster's cage, then heard the pernicious squeak of the Hamster's wheel. Turning, turning, turning, forever like the hands of a clock. There was no control of the Hamster's energy when it wanted to run. The Abacus filled his lungs. There were still uncounted things yet to say and he knew his words would cover the squeak of the Hamster's wheel like a band-aid over a bleeding wound.

'What about The Tablet?' said the voice from the cupboard.

All of the Abacus' beads darted from side to side in a frenzy. The Abacus threw his stick across the floor in a temper. It landed near the edge of the shelf, but then toppled over and fell towards the corner of the classroom. The Moon hid behind a cloud in the sky.

'The Tablet,' hissed the Abacus. '*The Screen that Screams*, that's what I call it. I tried to warn them. It's dangerous. Wild.

Evil. And it's a predator, waiting to be let out of his cage. Nobody can control it. It has the persuasion skills of a crooked politician and the energy of a million hamsters.'

The Hamster's wheel stopped. The Abacus looked across to see the Hamster was clinging to the side of his cage, his claws wrapped around the metal bars.

'Let me tell you what happens when you let The Tablet out of his cage,' said the Abacus, as he paused and squeezed his eyes shut. All the beads on the metal rods leaned to the right hand side and clicked together like magnets. 'It'll pounce on you playfully, lick your face like a dog, but then, when you're distracted, it'll sink its teeth into your subconscious and never let go.'

The Abacus watched the Hamster climb towards his water bottle, guzzle forty-nine sips of water, then retire to his nest of sawdust.

'Nobody wants to count with me,' mumbled the Abacus as his breathing slowed. His eyes closed, his head slowly cocked to one side to rest on his shoulder and his black toupee slipped off his head and fell to the floor.

A single yellow bead flicked from one side to the other, then another, and another. The beads on the Abacus' torso continued to count. The Tablet came out from the shadows of the stock cupboard and stood in front of the Abacus like a garden statue. The Tablet coaxed the Abacus to fall into its screen of enchanting colour and swim in the sea of stories that awaited him. The Abacus' beads continued to count, counting the number of forests that he was trekking through, counting the number of mountains that he was flying over, counting the number of clouds that he was dancing upon.

'How is this possible?' thought the Abacus.

The Tablet showed him stories of the Abacus helping thousands of children in thousands of classrooms in a thousand far-away lands. Lands with countless animals like lions and tigers and pandas and dragons.

'There's me!' exclaimed the Abacus. 'And me, and me, and me!' The Abacus kept on counting. The Tablet took the Abacus by the hand and flew him inside the head of one of the children.

'Another me!' said the Abacus as he watched a mirror image of himself, counting inside the imagination of the child. He watched as the child's finger pretended to flick abacus beads in mid-air on an imaginary abacus.

The Tablet powered down his screen and returned to the stock cupboard, leaving the Abacus sleeping on the shelf, his new memory of his ubiquitous presence comforting him like a warm blanket.

The Moon glided across the sky and tucked herself under the horizon, for it was time for the Sun to come up and start a new school day.

TWO DRAFTS

BY ANURAG

Wednesday
At Römer square,
In Frankfurt main,
A hundred chairs sit, empty,
Peacefully protesting
Against the autocracy,
Of being left in the open.
They crave to serve and be sat on,
Or at least to be kept inside.
It's been a sunny day,
Oh, a sunny day
Until now.
But now,
Clouds are taking over.
They fire drops.
It's minus fifteen.
Feels like minus fifty.
On their way down,
Drops turn into flakes of snow.
Clouds have not come alone,

A wild February wind approaches too,
From the sky and under the padlock bridge.
Chairs are helpless, hapless, lifeless.
They can't run, cry for mercy, resist.
They fall, one by one,
Oh, they could have been so much more,
Or someone else,
But they are just chairs,
A hundred empty chairs,
Black, woven in bamboo and mahogany
Defeated, fallen, now cremated in white, sinful snow
At the Romer square.

Sunday
At the Römer square
In Frankfurt main,
A hundred chairs have been crazy busy,
Being sat on, made into soccer goal posts.
Children run around, over, under them, cheering themselves,
squealing with joy.
It's been a sunny Sunday evening,
Waiters and waitresses run around them, cleaning tables,
Ignoring the chairs and the stains on them,
Of curry, coffee and other goddamned things.
Chairs don't even protest,
Tired by now
Of being left in open, of being sat upon.
It's been a sunny day,
Oh, a sunny day
Until now.
But now,
Clouds are taking over.
They fire drops.

It's minus fifteen.
Feels like minus fifty.
On their way down
Drops turn into flakes of snow,
Clouds have not come alone,
A wild February wind approaches too,
From the sky and under the padlock bridge
Chairs are helpless, and happy.
Unlike people,
They don't have to run, cry for mercy,
Or hide their faces in collars of their overcoats.
They fall, one by one, almost on purpose,
Overselling the wind.
Oh, they could have been so much more,
Or someone else,
But they are just chairs,
A hundred empty chairs,
Gladly so,
Black, woven in bamboo and mahogany,
Fallen, happily cremated under white flakes of snow
That have landed like angels upon their naked skins,
At the Römer square.

WHAT'S THE WORST THAT CAN HAPPEN?

BY ELENA VISO

Robert was silently cursing as he tried to adjust the delicate and expensive lab machine he pinched from his own scarce cash savings. He had built a lab in his guest room. Not an issue, it's not like he'd had any guests once he'd started this big project. Robert's skinny frame bent over the huge apparatus that was taking up almost the whole room.

'Right, just a bit to the left... come on... you stupid piece of second-hand equipment...'

With aching wrists, Robert tried to adjust a tiny wire. He'd been especially frustrated and angry for days, probably something to do with not being able to correctly set up his machine. But he wasn't much into self-analysis anymore. He also wasn't enjoying this project much. What was important was to spite his old colleagues, and everyone else, even that supermarket cashier from yesterday, who looked at him like he was a freak. Though maybe that last one was a little bit fair, looking at Robert's dishevelled hair and clothing for the wrong season, or even the wrong century.

It was everyone else's fault he was unhappy. Robert spiced that thought with some mock mumbling under his nose.

'Do this, do that, Robert. You're so smart, you have a PhD in Physics. Follow your dreams. No, creating a nuclear material experiment is not a good goal. You should consider leaving the Academy, Robert. It's best if you find other hobbies, Robert. Maybe you should take some time.' He sighed heavily. 'I'll give them *take some time*. None of them will have any research jobs left once my experiment succeeds.'

He was so tired of everything, of the shame and anger at having to abandon his previous work. Of his colleagues, who were keeping him at arm's length, and his few friends, who were happily moving ahead in life without him. But also, Robert needed to prove his family wrong. His standard middle class family, who already considered him a failure for pursuing an academic career.

'Because real men aren't loser pencil pushers, they either go build things or make money. What's the good of it if you're doing neither?' his father would say.

Robert went into science because there wasn't much else he was good at, certainly not at being active or social. And, surprise surprise, the Academy was all about being social. Precisely why he was back behind these closed doors.

'Come on... just a little bit to the left... I'm sure it'll work then. No chance of getting it wrong, not with my calculations.' Robert was desperately trying to connect the delicate wire into the main socket. 'If only I could get this last piece in, then it should...'

RIIIIING!!

A sharp noise pierced the silence. Robert dropped the wire as if it was on fire. He was vibrating from staying tense for so long and disoriented at what had just happened.

RIIIING!!

'Right, the doorbell.' He had almost forgotten the sound of it. Slowly, he crept down the corridor and glanced through the dusty eye in the door. As he opened the door, his guest didn't wait for a greeting.

'Hi, Mr Evans, nice to meet you again.' A man with a dark jacket that looked neither formal nor casual thrust a hand forward for a shake. 'We've met a couple of times during the annual Physics Symposium. I'm Steve Wellington from the Research Department.'

Robert eyed the visitor and, without shaking his hand, carefully stepped outside, closing the door behind his back.

'And?' he asked briskly. The vaguely familiar guy clearly knew him.

'And I just wanted to check whether you're still interested in continuing the particle research that you've been working on. Our department sent emails, but you never replied or confirmed your absence.'

Now, this was downright suspicious. First, those few emails looked more like spam, starting with *Dear Recipient*. Second, he was still vividly familiar with the strained environment among his colleagues, stuck in a place where no one could fire him, but no one wanted him around either. Robert was fairly sure it wasn't the reconnection that brought this unneeded guest here.

'What do you want?'

'As I said, we're following up on the research progress of our PhD students. If maybe we could go inside and chat for...'

'No!' Robert took a breath and spoke more evenly. 'No. I'm done here. You're not screwing up this research too, which, for your information, is private research.' He ripped the door open and slammed the door behind him without waiting for a reaction. Steve was left standing for several long minutes in the chilly wind. Eventually he pulled out his phone and dialled, still standing in Robert's doorway.

'Yes?' a rough voice picked up.

'Mr Johnston, I've just been to see Robert Evans.'

'And? How is he?'

'He's... well, not good...'

'Hah! Good!' The voice clearly cheered. 'I said all along we don't need him, waste of a good position as he was. Now I can write him off the list for good, and he might not even notice.'

'Is it really necessary? He mentioned he's working on something new...'

'Whatever. Better than that, I'll need you to find a new student for his position. Female and from a third world country – then I can tick the diversity box. Try to look among disability applicants; it'll bring us a bit of extra cash too. Then I can start looking for the students I really need. My alumni had several good recommendations.'

'Right...' Steve was listening, with furrowed brows. 'And you're absolutely sure?'

'Absolutely. Anyway, what's the worst that can happen?'

A sudden flash of light and heat ripped through the air, as the voice still rang through the phone speaker, carrying an explosion that was too quick to allow Steve to react. Too powerful to even spare the street, or the next street. Or the whole town, for that matter, with the Academy and Johnston's office in it. A nuclear experiment gone wrong: starting in Robert's guest room, it had, in mere seconds, cleaned the whole coastal town off the ground.

Printed in Poland
by Amazon Fulfillment
Poland Sp. z o.o., Wrocław